ONCE IN A BLUE MOON

Joshua Parapuram

MINERVA PRESS
LONDON
MIAMI RIO DE JANEIRO DELHI

ONCE IN A BLUE MOON
Copyright   Joshua Parapuram 2000

All Rights Reserved

ISBN 0 75411 268 3

First Published 2000 by
MINERVA PRESS
315–317 Regent Street
London W1R 7YB

Printed in Great Britain for Minerva Press

ONCE IN A BLUE MOON

As stated in the foreword, this is a work of fiction and all characters and situations are purely imaginary. I have taken liberties with geography and avoided getting entangled in the intricacies of what is, after all, an extremely complex military operation. The fact that the action takes place 'some years into the new millennium' is intended to establish that political and military leaders of the present time have all exited the scene before the drama unfolds.

To Susy

Some men see things as they are and ask why.
I dream of things that never were and ask why not.

George Bernard Shaw

Foreword

This is fiction. The story of an event some years into the new millennium. Malaysia plods on in the wake of the schism created by the Anwar Ibrahim saga[1]. But it is a rich country. While the Singaporeans try to break out of the timidity imposed by many years of authoritarianism, the republic remains far more economically powerful, and its people dare to dream a bigger dream[2]. I hope this will be read as a cautionary tale.

---

[1]   Anwar Ibrahim was Malaysia's Deputy Prime Minister until he was unceremoniously dumped by Prime Minister Dr Mahathir Mohamad, in 1998. There followed a sensational and salacious trial which saw him convicted and sentenced to six years' jail on charges of abusing his powers to quash allegations of sexual misconduct. Those allegations led to another trial in which Anwar was accused of committing sodomy, and further allegations of corruption remained unresolved. These events were accompanied by sporadic public protests, amidst suspicions of a set-up to thwart a leadership challenge, as alleged by Anwar's supporters.

[2]   In 1998 the International Water Management Institute based in Sri Lanka predicted that in twenty-five years, one-third of the world's population would be in serious trouble because of water shortage.

About the Author

Joshua Parapuram has worked as a journalist in Singapore and Malaysia for many years. At seventeen he joined *The Straits Times* in Singapore as a cadet reporter. The year was 1953, and nascent nationalism in Singapore and Malaya was becoming vocal in a British colonial environment. Parapuram observed the rise of the People's Action Party and its leader Lee Kuan Yew as a potent political force in Singapore and the region.

Parapuram has also been editor of the *Malay Mail* in Kuala Lumpur, and worked with News Ltd in Sydney. He now works as a sub-editor on *The Straits Times* in Sydney.

Chapter One

The same cocky, loping walk, the head a little more shiny. Tessy's face burst into the same old big-mouthed smile.

'Dom Thomas!'

The two men stood on the pavement outside the hotel beaming at each other; the moment bridged thirty-five years. Dom had stepped out of the hotel during a twenty-four hour stopover, debating where to go for lunch, left towards Chinatown or right towards Orchard Road.

'This must mean something. If the timing had been off a minute we wouldn't have met,' Dom told his friend.

The new Singapore shone like a jewel in the brilliant morning sunshine. It would get hot and muggy later, but at this moment all was well with the world.

It was not the Singapore that Dom and Tessy had known. The city had a virtual feel about it, the glass and steel and concrete all fitting together so perfectly. The people seemed to be out of place. Still, Dom and Tessy were young again, and Dom could see in his mind's eye the old Rendezvous coffee shop opposite the Cathay cinema where they used to gather for Sunday lunch, hot Indonesian fare with cold Anchor beer. The Washington, the International, the popular pubs of the time, were all gone, together with the ancient buildings in Bras Basah Road, in the city's constant renewal. Vanished into history or dispersed into dark caverns in the innards of the concrete jungle that is modern Singapore.

Dom was the only one allowed to call his old friend Tessy, for Texeira. Frederick Alonso Texeira's father was the progeny of a Portuguese seafarer and an Indian nurse, and his mother the daughter of a Chinese trader in Mindanao and a Filipino salesgirl. The true South-East Asian, and his identity card proclaimed his race as Eurasian.

After the hugs and backslapping Tessy asked, 'How much

time you spending in Singapore?'

'Just a twenty-four hour stopover. I am leaving tonight.'

'You know my brother is in Internal Security. He's been telling the relatives not to go out unnecessarily and to stock up on food. So I think some kind of fireworks is in the pipeline.'

'Fireworks?'

'Just a guess, but I think it could be military. A lot of national servicemen have been called up for a range of activities like refresher courses, equipment upgrading and the like. Just window dressing. Something big's about to happen.'

A flash of worry creased his brow, and his mouth twisted in a mirthless smile.

The last time Dom had seen that look was during the Hock Lee riots in the 50s. He had gone out to have a look at what all the excitement was about and had found himself on the wrong side of the communist-inspired rampage by students and bus company workers, which had been brutally put down by the colonial police. He had barely escaped from the howling mob, and had worn a haunted look for days.

'What is it?'

There was an urgency in Dom's question.

'As I said, it could be military. Can't imagine what sort. Nothing to worry you Aussies.'

Dom noticed the extra emphasis on the last word, but decided to ignore it. Many of his friends still believed his migration to Australia was a mistake.

Tessy broke the pause.

'Come, I have a surprise for you.'

Tessy took Dom to lunch at the Rendezvous, now relocated at the nearby Raffles Centre. Dom recognised only the name, for the reincarnation was beyond comprehension. The coffee shop ambience had given way to linen service and waiters in black tie and white jackets, each one with an ostentatious, immaculately white and starched napkin on his left sleeve, probably reflecting Singapore's own metamorphosis. They ordered their old favourites – the beef, the chicken, the hot fish curry, the *blachan* greens.

Dom wondered if the 'fireworks' that Tessy had spoken about

would disrupt his onward flight. He could move in with his cousin, one of several relatives Dom had in Singapore. It was off-season, so changing flights should not be a problem. He wanted to yarn a little with his old friend; more importantly, he did not want to miss the 'fireworks' if there were going to be any.

'Do you have a favourite pub these days?' Dom asked.

'Well, yes. It's not too flashy, but I like the guy who runs it. Don't know if you remember him. Fatso Fong, from Rochore Road. He's not doing too well because the young guys don't go to pubs like Fatso's. They want to be seen in fancy places with fancy prices.'

They walked back to the hotel together and Dom checked out; then he called his cousin to say he would be turning up at his doorstep some time during the evening, but not to wait up for him. He left his suitcase in Tessy's car and the two walked on to Fatso Fong's. As they ordered the first beers of what looked like a long, long session, other orders, purely military, were being issued elsewhere in Singapore. And more code words for a national service call-up appeared on the television screen: *Green Field, Red Sand, Fruit Tree, Steel Door, Blue Bird, Big Wheel, Mango Tree, Uncle John, Zinc Shed, Sand Hill, Water Bottle, Green Leaf, Night Shade, Orchid Corner, Star Light, Street Corner.* It was going to be a long night.

★

Ah Kong waved away the persistent mosquito and looked out to sea again. His tiny eyes were red and his head hurt. He was running out of fresh water and bug spray, and he had to watch out for falling coconuts. He felt exposed on the stretch of sand on the Johore coast that had been his home for over a fortnight.

At 5 a.m. he had called a number on his mobile phone, as he had done every day since he arrived, and every morning the message had been the same. He had reached a disconnected number. But today it had been different. The message was just one word, repeated over and over: *Temasek, Temasek, Temasek.*

Many others in the field of operations, like Ah Kong, were getting the same message. His cracked lips struggled to smile –

Tora, Tora, Tora? Images of the Japanese attack on Hawaii flashed before his eyes. But he was not looking up into the sky: he was looking out to sea.

Then he saw them. Out of the east, with the morning sun, came growing dots on the horizon, dots that grew into scores and scores of small pleasure craft, joined by more coming south and north along the shoreline. Ah Kong knew then that the military operation to secure Singapore's water supplies, unfortunately in a foreign, increasingly hostile country, had really begun. His job was done; he could leave.

He had worked alone, just an *ah kong* or grandfather in Hokkien, marking out three routes into the plantations and the jungle for the men gathering in groups on the beach. All the military hardware had been moved in secretly and cached away, but not everyone knew where exactly they were. He had them all pinpointed, and he showed them the way.

★

There were no barking orders on the beach, not much conversation either. Everyone knew what was to be done, and they moved into the mix of coconut, rubber and oil palm plantations and jungle, following routes marked by coloured plastic strips. They would find the guns, ammo, mortar launchers and hand-held rocket launchers that can bring down aircraft and helicopters – everything for a military operation that would create a defence line, coast to coast, north of the catchment areas supplying Singapore's water.

The boats that had brought almost 1,000 men were already dispersing in all directions and Ah Kong waded out and swam the short distance to the Katong-cat which had been lingering to pick up just the one passenger. Lieutenant Colonel Tan Hee Kean could now revert to his real name and rank, but that was not uppermost on his mind.

★

Sleep, glorious unconsciousness. He was already snoring as the small boat turned her head for home. On a giant wall map back in the Blue Room, the nerve centre of an underground network off Bukit Timah Road in the rocky heart of the island of Singapore, applause broke out as the beginnings of a red dotted line on the Johore coast began to appear. That line would extend south, then west, with slight variations for the lay of the land, as the day progressed. The air force was already in action to stop Malaysian forces moving south. A small contingent would be disarming Malaysian police, immigration, and customs personnel at both crossing points, at Tuas and Woodlands. All Malaysian armed personnel south and east of a line Mersing south to Jemaluang, west to Keluang, then Batu Pahat on the Straits of Malacca would be ordered to hand in their weapons at the nearest police station and go home. Taking prisoners was not top of the agenda, but everyone had to stay out of the way. Meanwhile, the thin red line would continue to snake its way to the west coast. The line would have to hold.

In later years, military strategists would marvel at the novelty of the operation. A seaborne invasion had been effected without gunfire, and the men had all gone in wearing casual clothes. Most of the action, if any at this early stage, would take place out of sight in plantations and jungle. But video and still pictures were coming through to Mindef, or the Ministry of Defence, in a steady stream, for technology had made any war accessible. Frontline coverage was also going to the Blue Room, but its members were more interested in the air strikes.

South-East Asia would never be the same again. National borders and politics, population movements and economic growth, the old status quo of Malay-Chinese co-existence, everything now assumed new perspectives with one powerful display of the strength of the Singapore dollar over the Malaysian ringgit and the Indonesian rupiah; the first bud of the final flowering of the Singapore story, the unspoken wish, the recurring dream of Singaporeans that one day they could stop being nice to people who did not like them, just because these people controlled their water supply. Notwithstanding their money, sophistication and culture, a proud people were clearly squirming in their upholstered seats. It was the water. Any other annoyance they could cope with. But not a threat to their water supply. Plainly unfriendly acts and statements that would otherwise have been slapped aside or simply ignored had to be rationalised, pride swallowed, shoulders shrugged and everyone reminded to keep their minds on the main game. They had to give face to people they had little respect for. They needed time to put on some real muscle until the new dawn when all slights would be repaid in full measure and Singapore would again be in full control of her own destiny. With plenty of land and water. So one could stretch one's arms a bit. And legs. And dream bigger dreams.

The dawn of the new millennium had brought new and more strident frictions with Malaysia. Military thinking had begun to veer towards the possibility of armed conflict following the little spat with Malaysia in 1998 over the railway line and the unnecessary difficulties over moving the customs and immigration checkpoints for railway passengers from Tanjong Pagar in the far south of the island to Woodlands up north near the crossing point at the Causeway, the old land bridge across the tiny strip of water separating the island republic of Singapore from peninsular Malaysia.

In the midst of that furore, the Malaysian Prime Minister, Dr Mahathir, had called an anti-Singapore rally in Johore Bahru and the crowd had shouted, 'Cut, cut, cut,' referring to the water. Each 'Cut!' had sent a shiver down the spine of Singaporeans watching the television news.

The level of bitterness and hatred manifested at the time reconfirmed what Lee Kuan Yew had called an irreparable fault line in the Malay-Chinese relationship. With the Malays in control in Malaysia and the Chinese in control in Singapore, a military confrontation had always appeared a likelihood; and Mindef, over time, had refreshed and revived war models from discs filed away long ago. The prospect was that the water supply would get mired in endless negotiations with cries of 'cut' every now and then, and that the population would become increasingly jittery.

Considering the rhetoric emanating from Malaysian politicians, anything was possible, even a sudden armed conflict, and a thinking person would wonder whether that should also be the occasion to take steps to safeguard one's water supply. Well, then, if circumstances permitted, why not take the pre-emptive option? What would those circumstances be that would allow overt military action, keeping in mind what happened to Iraq and Saddam over Kuwait, and Milosovic over Kosovo? That was a thought that worried Tan, as it did many others in Singapore, including members of the Blue Room.

Coincidentally, the political instability in Malaysia that had begun with the inept sacking, detention under the draconian Internal Security Act and prosecution of Mahathir's number two, Anwar Ibrahim, on corruption and sodomy charges, had also begun in 1998, one of the important factors that had contributed to Singapore's belief that the chips were beginning to fall in its favour for a military strike.

*

Just about the time that Singapore troops were moving off the Mersing beaches, the beautiful Stella Chin was again allowing herself to be seduced by a politician who had some weight in the Johore State Assembly. The eventual role that Singapore wanted Jaffar Ibrahim to be persuaded to perform was to make pro-Singapore noises so that the Sultan would jump the right way. That was the key to a bigger play. Could the Sultan be tempted with the title of President of Singapore, in addition to Sultan of Johore? Another imponderable, for the idea had not been broached with the ruler yet, because premature disclosure could have disastrous consequences. So Stella kept up the good work. But today it had been difficult for Jaffar to get away. There was the scream of jets and the runway bombings, effectively leaving the entire RMAF (Royal Malaysian Air Force) unable to take off. The phones were jammed, both terrestrial and satellite. The mobile phone was dropping out within seconds. But Stella was a prize too good to pass up. Events beyond his control were unfolding, and Jaffar could not understand what exactly was going on. He would know in due course, he told himself, but in the meantime there was no point in wasting time worrying about it.

The same thought was on Stella's mind. Her own job would reach some sort of conclusion soon. The bodies she could see in the mirror on the dressing table looked like other people's. She could detach herself and even admire those two bodies; they seemed to fit each other so well. She found that their intrigue added extra spice to their lovemaking.

From the very beginning it had never been an unpleasant experience for her, maybe even pleasurable; for the tallish man with the beginnings of a paunch, grey at the temples and with two deep lines on either side of his nose had that distinguished bearing, the Dato look, that comes from moderate indulgence and supreme self-confidence. For Jaffar, his faith in himself was justified now, with this beautiful woman who had fallen into his lap with very little persuasion. Stella was being adequately rewarded, of course. Jaffar did not need to know that; the money would be credited into her DBS bank account. Still, what if the thing became public knowledge? She would die of shame. But on the other hand…

Stella had been a waitress in Singapore, a trolley-girl in a *yum-cha* place, until she had been discovered by a police officer and recommended to Internal Security. Discovered, in the sense that she fitted a personality profile prepared for a special project. For Stella, it all began when she answered a telephone call to go for an interview in Fullerton Square – supposedly something to do with her troublesome boyfriend, Bob. The well-dressed woman sitting behind the huge desk seemed to know everything about Stella, and told her that she wanted to speak to her about something very special; and Stella was told about people who were sometimes called upon to perform patriotic duties beyond the humdrum of normal existence.

Stella was plainly excited as Ms Choo, for that was what the woman said her name was, continued to speak, a pleasant, lilting voice totally out of place with the austere, institutional furniture in the room. Stella heard about the good-looking Jaffar, how lucky she, Stella, was to be born with such good looks as to be able to convince him to work for Singapore's national interests. She would be guided and advised as the matter progressed, and she would have the help and guidance of many unseen people who would be looking out for her. It would be an adventure no girl would want to turn down – good clothes, good grooming, and good money. It was put across to her in an indirect way much later in the piece that she might have to sleep with Jaffar, but by then she was ready for anything.

The proposition was simple enough, and Bob's name never came up during the discussion, except that she was not to have anything more to do with him. Stella could see right away that this was the break she had always fantasised she would get one day. She would win a beauty contest, land an acting role on television, make a Canto-pop hit, maybe even win the lottery. Or something. And she would fly high. Bob Ng was never going to be anything much. All he ever wanted was to go to bed with her. She was tired of the cheap-eats and stall food, and she never knew what he actually did for a living; something to do with taxis, she was told, although he was not a driver. She should have done better in school. Her dad was retired, all his life a meticulous but low-paid clerk in the museum; mum had never worked. Stella was an only child, and there were constant discussions with relatives about what Stella was going to do. Here, now, was her chance to be a heroine straight out of a Hong Kong movie. *Mata Hari*! It was a pleasurable thought.

*

Stella moaned, pulled Jaffar's hair, and relapsed into a dazed state as he began to pant. If Bob knew what she was up to. Doing her duty! It really didn't matter that Stella hadn't gone beyond her O levels. She had taken small jobs as a waitress and sales assistant, and drifted into a relationship with Bob. Once in a while they would discuss marriage; that would make it easy to get a Housing Board flat he had said. But Stella had wondered if she wasn't meant for better things. She was aware that she was blessed with beautiful skin and lovely hair; never mind her slightly squishy face. Her nose was a little broad, her eyes a little top-heavy, her full lips tended to droop at the ends giving her a sad look, and her teeth had a thousand fillings. She had always thought her boobs were small, and had a habit of stuffing tissues in her bra, although

Bob had never remarked on their size. And she had this habit of flicking her hair back that made her appear rude or impatient. It had always bugged Bob. Still, no serious flaws; nothing that a flash of thigh could not overcome.

Stella made a few more noises to let Jaffar know that she was not entirely out of the action. He squeezed her: it hurt. She moved, to present a better angle for the hidden video camera, which now had Jaffar's face in full.

He uttered a moan and fell in a heap, then he looked up briefly and smiled, Stella's glowing expression giving him reaffirmation of the power of his charisma, and he drifted to sleep.

She pulled herself from under him and made for the bathroom. She would be gone by the time he got up, and they would not meet again until he called her. Probably in a week's time, as had been their practice for the past few weeks. But what effect was all this military activity going to have on their meetings? Jaffar was thinking the same thing. He would not give her up easily. Each time they met he felt six feet tall.

He had always been lucky with women, but they were all of a certain type; nothing like this sophisticated businesswoman who bad come to him seeking his help with a land development application, and things had progressed beautifully from there. They hardly ever talked about that application any more. It suited him just fine. It was Stella who rented the house where they met, to prevent embarrassment for the politician. It remained empty at other times, except for this other woman that Stella had arranged to clean the place and change the sheets – and take away the video tape.

★

Lieutenant Colonel Tan woke up with a start, although the sea was calm and the Katong-cat was purring along fairly smoothly. The old fears had returned. The sweat poured from his face. Was there something they had overlooked? All this talk of the Singapore story; had it all been a purely ethnic Chinese enterprise, sustained and prosecuted by the Chinese diaspora right across South-East Asia and further afield? He remembered Dr

Wong sounding a warning that the face of Singapore should always be presented as one of many cultural and racial origins, which meant the non-Chinese should be given sufficient exposure in all echelons of government, however strong traditional Chinese prejudices might be. The Malay and South Asian presence, however small, needed to be accommodated to avoid the Chinese chauvinistic stigma.

The government-run newspapers and television and radio could all be targeted at serving the Chinese market, for ethnic Chinese made up the vast majority of the population – and voters. The others simply had to accept this reality. No non-Chinese could ever expect to become Prime Minister, and no one in their right mind would either. There were some non-Chinese throughout the political, professional and bureaucratic spheres. Tokenism was obvious, but then something is always better than nothing. And, in Singapore, that something was quite something by Asian standards.

The small Indian, Sri Lankan and Eurasian communities accepted being left outside the main centres of power, but the Malays had never fully accepted their status of being outsiders in what they regarded as their island, for Malays were the original inhabitants; all the others came later as immigrants. What was more, across the Causeway on the peninsula, Malays ruled the land, with control of the army, navy, air force, police, the bureaucracy and parliament; and now significant sections of commercial and business activity were also moving into Malay hands.

The Colonel, looking out to sea from a porthole on the Katong-cat, was certain that Malay resentment would be running deep in Singapore, never mind the fury in Malaysia. Many others were worried too, not least in the Blue Room, where the ubiquitous Dr Wong would be peering at arrays of computer monitors. The respected scholar and government adviser had been the last to give way to the hawks, for he looked on the history of South-East Asia in slightly different terms than the patently chauvinistic manner of some of his peers. He remembered visiting the national museum in Kuala Lumpur, and his comrade from the old days, when he used to dabble in the virtues of socialism, had pointed out the bronze of a legendary warrior from Malacca called Hang Tuah, with the engraved words *Tak Melayu Hilang Di Dunia – The Malays Shall Not Vanish From The World*, the core of Malay consciousness. Every inch of land would be held sacred by these people.

★

The men in the Blue Room were also aware that a military action would be resisted, unless overwhelming power persuaded Malaysia's political leaders to give way and decide to fight another day. The fighting spirit of the Malay soldier had never been truly tested since the jungle-war days against poorly-armed communist insurgents and clumsy Indonesian infiltrators a long time ago.

Even as the Colonel's thoughts drifted to his wife waiting anxiously in their twenty-first storey flat in Thomson Road, RSAF (Republic of Singapore Air Force) F-16C/Ds and new generation F-15s and F-18s were returning to Tengah and Sembawang air force bases. The attack had been relatively easy because all of Malaysia's fighting aircraft, a polyglot force of Russian, British and American-made aircraft, had been gathered at Kuantan air base on the east coast and the Subang domestic airport near Kuala Lumpur for a celebratory inspection and fly-past.

And an impressive sight they made too. The old air base out-side of the city in Sungei Besi contained only the RMAF's transports and helicopters. Singapore strike aircraft had cratered runways at Subang and Kuantan, effectively bottling up the Malaysian air force. Singapore's E-2C Hawkeye early warning aircraft cruised up and down the east coast, and Singapore's newly acquired F-117As patrolled the Straits of Malacca, shepherded by two KC-135 mid-air refuelling tankers. Four RMAF training aircraft which were in the air at the time had been escorted down to land at Tengah. Air power was the key.

★

Everything was going according to plan. The huge media

campaign was being orchestrated efficiently, prudently mixed with five-star hospitality for the hordes of media representatives that had begun to converge on Singapore. Sound bites, action footage, maps, graphs and a steady flow of what the world wanted to hear. It was a pre-emptive, relatively low-casualty action to prevent a campaign of ethnic cleansing about to be launched by Malay forces against the Chinese segment of Malaysia's population.

There was, of course, a history of racial violence in Malaysia and Indonesia. Only recently, there had been the horrendous attacks on ethnic Chinese in Indonesia, also made up of people of the same stock as the Malays. And Indonesia's East Timor fiasco still lingered in Asian minds. The lessons were obvious for shrewd people on both sides of the Causeway. Perceptions would be important.

*

The seeds of the fear of racial unrest had always been there in Malaysia-Singapore relations. And somehow it appeared easier to believe Singapore officials than the Malaysian leadership which had at some time or other offended sensibilities in most of the centres of power and, more importantly, the foreign media. Satellite news reports had been interrupted by Malaysian officials the last time something politically newsworthy happened in KL – the Anwar Ibrahim saga. The police chief had acted boorishly at a news conference ('You shut up,' he had told a British journalist) and had been lampooned in the overseas media. Anwar's black eye and bruises when he appeared in court had antagonised even more people, including political leaders in the region. A swipe at currency speculators and Jews by Dr Mahathir over the ringgit's sinking value was only the tip of the long-standing anti-Israeli sentiment in the Malaysian government, most of whose members were devout Muslims. That had put the Americans offside, and the sour note had continued to poison relations between the two countries.

And there had always been rumours of Israeli assistance for Singapore in military affairs. The national service mechanism was said to be based on the Israeli model. There was the time when people on both sides of the Causeway enjoyed the joke over the large numbers of *gwei-lo* (round-eyes) that had suddenly appeared in Singapore streets and were explained away as 'Mexican tourists'. They had been, actually, Israeli military personnel.

★

Nick Cohen wanted to speak to Dr Wong urgently. The phone went unattended at his home. Even the answering machine was not on. He appeared to be uncontactable. The Americans had been watching the unfolding scenario with growing alarm. Surprise that Singapore had actually gone and done it was giving way to a feeling that China had somehow outflanked American influence. Cohen, a political analyst, had been in the Singapore embassy only six months as part of his training for bigger things in the foreign service.

Anyone could have foreseen the breakout of hostilities if only one knew where to look. Singapore's acquisition of airborne early warning aircraft, the mid-air refuelling tankers, the so-called 'bunker-buster bombs', the national service call-up as part of a preparedness exercise, civil defence exercises, rationing exercises, the increasing level of armaments on military aircraft, the jingoistic language of some politicians... Then there were the unexplained absences of political leaders. They were, in fact, spending a lot of time in the Blue Room, so called because of a surfeit of blue lighting in corridors and annexes, or it could have been for the Blue Light Laser communications web that left a faint halo over the entire area despite heavy masking techniques.

It had sixty full members, and their nominated proxies and aides, representing power in Singapore, from banking, finance, academia, clan associations, and political and military leaders – all chosen by consensus to decide the future of the immigrant presence in South-East Asia, bunkered deep down in the granite heart of the island. There were two square kilometres of tunnels, halls and sophisticated electronics, approached from inconspicuous lanes off Bukit Timah and Dunearn Roads.

Everyone knew about the underground project, including

Cohen, but not its extent or true intent. There were similar underground projects elsewhere, in Russia, China, Iran and North Korea in particular. It was known that the North Koreans developed, tested and deployed the No Dong missile without anyone having a clue; and all was made possible with the development of boring machines that make a fifteen by sixty metre hole in a day. Singapore had four toiling day and night.

Cohen was also aware that the mighty *USS Harry S. Truman* had quietly moved into the South China Sea. Did the Pentagon know something that he did not? Was he not made privy because of his new girlfriend?

Janet Lim had drifted into his life and she was spending a lot of time in his company. All night and most of the day too. And he had this problem with the First Secretary. The day after he arrived the creep had told him another Cohen joke.

'Hey, Nick, heard the one about this Cohen who married a Spanish lass? They had a daughter and they named her Carmen. Dad insisted on calling her Cohen and Mom would only call her Carmen. After a while the poor kid didn't know whether she was Carmen or Cohen.'

Funny ha ha. *I'll get him for that one day*, Cohen had told himself. But he had more pressing things on his mind.

Janet called to go for lunch. She was, in fact, in the lobby. She was also worried about her extended family in Malaysia, for the Lim family wealth had been built on Malaysian tin and then partly moved into property in Singapore. Her brother was a senior official in the Foreign Investment Bureau, selling the Singapore dream of unmatched profits to investors all over the world. He needed to know something, and she had to do it for him. She should ask her boyfriend what the *Truman* was doing so close to the action.

That had never been in Singapore's calculations, for the diplomats and ministers had been at pains to persuade the Americans of their loyalty to Western ideals, with appropriate modifications for Asian sensibilities. Singapore was doing what it had to do only for self-preservation, to save capitalism, meritocracy and multiculturalism from religious fanatics. And, of course, to pre-empt a bloody bout of ethnic cleansing. Words that should resonate sympathetically in the American Congress.

The *Truman*'s appearance was disturbing, regardless of the neutral noises coming from Washington. Had they not done something like this to Saddam? Given him enough rope to hang himself? Some inkling had to be discovered in a roundabout way. No point in asking straight questions. Who was it who said that you should not ask questions if you did not want to hear lies?

Diplomats go about it in different ways, like persuading a target's girlfriend to ask the difficult questions. She did, and Cohen began to suspect that some things were going over his head. He was on the phone asking questions, and getting told to back off. There was nothing going on, as far as American forces were concerned, except that the *Truman* happened to be there as part of its global tour of duty.

Just then, Singapore television interrupted the Chinese movie with another Important Statement by a Defence Ministry spokesman, that Singapore forces were progressing satisfactorily in the Johore operation. Cohen phoned Janet in the lobby and told her that he was unable to step out of the office, that she should go straight home, to his flat, and wait for him. Neither knew that it was going to be a long day.

What bothered Cohen was that, to his knowledge, their satellites had not picked up the seaborne action. The two satellites had missed the whole thing. Not difficult, really. It had been done before, notably by the Indians when they conducted those nuclear tests. Or had the American military known in advance and pretended not to see? The explanation would be that this was not an area of particular military interest; that there were other areas of intense concern. And movements by elements of the Chinese army, navy and air force were sending increasingly confused signals; and now you were talking about mega-bombs and delivery systems. And there had been tensions at the seams in the world's largest dictatorship accompanied by a dilution of central control. There had been questions in the Pentagon about exactly who had their finger on China's nuclear trigger. Unhappy parallels with the dismantling of the Soviet empire had been remarked upon in several studies.

Cohen called his old university friend, Tony Bradley, at the

State Department, who was privy to most things because of the nature of his work in the records section. Bradley knew why the *Truman* was where it was, but he couldn't tell Cohen. Everything he said on the phone was being recorded as a matter of routine, and this was too big for the likes of Cohen. If Cohen's own colleagues hadn't told him, he, Bradley, was not going to do so. He told his friend that the *Truman* was simply monitoring the situation. Hostilities of this nature had not taken place in that part of the world since the Indonesian Confrontation against the old Malaya and the British.

'We are anxious that the thing doesn't draw in other countries,' Bradley told his friend. 'That's the limit of our interest.'

That was partly true.

Janet called again. Sorry, he was going to be late.

'It's the red satin today,' she told him, and she knew the effect it usually had on him.

Red satin underwear and a certain way of sitting on the sofa. Cohen had his weaknesses, and Janet knew them all.

She had mastered her wiles in Hong Kong as a property tycoon's *tai-tai*; the man had gone bust and she had been left with nothing. She had her new opportunities in Singapore only because her brother had been kind enough to forgive her transgressions and arrange for her to get a regular income from the family fortune.

Janet put on the red satin stuff and looked at herself in the full-length mirror on the bedroom wall. A tallish woman in her early thirties, with closely bobbed hair, and with a sensual face bearing the fuller eyes of the *nyonya*, or Straits Chinese.

'I've still got it,' she told herself, turning sideways to see the profile of her breasts and the curve of her back.

Her figure was the type that demanded red satin underwear, and she felt recharged and empowered as she lay on the bed; Cohen would be turning up any minute now. She was going to give him a pleasant surprise.

Chapter Two

As Lieutenant Soh Ming Tung gathered his men on the beach, the town of Mersing was just waking up. The skippers of the myriad boats and cruisers that made up the Singapore invasion force had been under strict instructions not to go up the *sungei*, or river – that short stretch of which was to be part of the new border.

Soh and his men had a special assignment. They were to equip themselves and proceed to the town, on the south bank, and disarm the small police contingent. There was nothing much else to do there. The town was to be allowed to function as normal. There would be boats tied up on the muddy bank which took holidaymakers to the small island of Tioman.

His orders were to avoid casualties, and the people were not to be molested or treated cruelly. 'We are a benevolent force. We hope to be greeted with cheers and open arms,' he had been told. But he did not hear many cheers; he was confronted with fearful faces and an unspoken accusation that the lives of the townspeople had taken an unpredictable turn not of their choosing.

There was also disbelief. The very thought of an invasion force, that from tiny Singapore, was so outlandish. Singapore, with a population of just over three million, was taking on Malaysia, population eighteen million. The truth would be out soon enough; but it was worrying that the Malay constabulary had all been sent home, without their weapons.

A couple of Singapore soldiers could be seen inside the police station, one pacing the inspector's room with a telephone stuck to his ear. Soh decided that there was no immediate need for a curfew, but the bridge had to be blockaded and placed sentries to guard against infiltration across the river. Boats coming downriver from the fishing villages had to be monitored, but headquarters reckoned that there would be no attack from the Malaysians in this area because of the swamps and muddy creeks. If anything, action would come west of Keluang, the small town in the centre of the line linking Jemaluang to Batu Pahat on the other coast.

The fall-back line was Mersing south to Kota Tinggi, west to Kulai, then to Pontian Kecil on the west coast. In the event of a massive ground attack, Singapore troops would retreat to this second line, and the area in between would be the kill zone. Big guns had been set up in the south, and targeting was in full swing. Singapore's full military capabilities would be used in this sector, for there was to be no going back to the island. The battle would have to be fought and won here. Singapore as a battleground was inconceivable.

*

The guard swung open the heavy iron gates, and the driver took the Merc right up the driveway of the large house in one of Singapore's more salubrious postcodes. The old Chinese maid who opened the door announced to the gathering in the lounge in Cantonese that Dr Wong was at the door, completely ignoring the other man with him.

Dr Wong Meng Kwang, a history scholar and economist in his early fifties with thick glasses, receding hairline, a pear-shaped body and a round face with a permanently startled look, turned to his friend; but before he spoke, Dr Selva Rajah told him, 'Never mind, Doc. You don't have to apologise for that silly woman.'

Those sorts of casual slights were prevalent with Singapore's ascent to become one of the Asian Tigers, while countries in South Asia, especially, sank into a mess of their own making. From the Khyber Pass to the Pacific, apart from Japan and South Korea, the bright spots were Hong Kong, Taiwan and Singapore. The others had all screwed up their economies by years of apathy and intellectual bankruptcy, interrupted by brief moments of prosperity. China was the powerhouse, while India, Pakistan, Bangladesh and Sri Lanka blundered on under the weight of religious and caste divisions. Those countries had actually been excluded from some of Asia's highest councils like the Europe-Asia economic summit and Apec; a pointed snub well understood in Asia.

Dr Wong had taken the Indian GP along for his, Dr Wong's, own protection, for Dr Selva Rajah, a long-time confidante of the Prime Minister, had certain security functions; and it was always good to have someone else with you on these sensitive visits. The man they were visiting, Tjong Ming Seng, an Indonesian tycoon and acknowledged leader of the network of expatriate Chinese investors in Singapore, came up to them with outstretched arms.

'Come in, come into my humble abode.'

Dr Rajah noted the man's sense of humour, for the house was almost as big as the Presidential Istana, or palace.

Dr Wong said, 'Hello, everybody.'

And the others said, 'Hello, Dr Wong,' and retreated to the large veranda.

Another Important Statement was on the television. A pretty Indian girl read from a text, then a map showed the state of Johore with a red dotted line heading across it from Mersing to the other coast, without anything being said about what that line was. There was no mention of casualties, only that roads in Singapore were expected to be opened to civilian traffic the following morning, depending on developments during the night. And there was no mention of forces moving up on the two main arteries going north from Tuas and Woodlands. The stock exchange had not opened at all. It was a Friday, providing a cooling-off period until at least Monday.

Dr Wong came to the point quickly.

'The Prime Minister wants to know what your reaction is.'

'Maybe we could have talked some more,' said Tjong.

'Yes, of course. But we had come to the conclusion that further discussions were fruitless. And that this was the right time to act, if we intended to act at all. Have you heard anything from Jakarta?' asked Dr Wong.

'They are angry like hell, but I don't think they will do anything about it. I am sure KL is in touch, and Othman is having a difficult time explaining why ABRI is doing nothing. Well, nothing more than some jumping up and down, and maybe even some sponsored disturbances. The Chinese community will again be the target, but this time the Chinese are not offering much of a target. They have all gone out of sight. Their old shops were not really repaired after the last riots, the ones that brought down Soeharto. So damage will be limited.'

Nothing new there. Dr Wong had seen the Institute of Strategic Studies assessment. He wanted to know whether Tjong and his mates would pull out their money from Singapore banks. The belief in the Blue Room was *no*, but a report from the Monetary Authority noted some large-scale movements – not just Western fund managers in the fray, but many Asian players moving out physical cash. Stocks and bonds and derivatives were not seriously affected because there was an unwillingness to bear the loss while head office was saying that the situation would correct itself fairly quickly.

'*Tiew nia seng!*' the tycoon swore quietly. 'So really my money is all you want. Not my advice, ah?'

Dr Wong laughed. He hadn't heard such obscenities in a long time.

'Yes and no, lah. You know how it is. We depend on people like you to provide confidence in the marketplace.'

'Okay. The fact is, I did my business last week,' conceded Tjong.

'You knew?'

'Yes, and no, lah. A good guess. Even with friends like you, I had to do all the hard work myself to find out what was going on. And I took a few prudent steps. The market is closed today. You know that.'

'Yes. The real reason I came was to ask you about the other business. I didn't want to use the phone,' said Dr Wong. The businessman looked at the tall Indian man.

'He can hear what you have to say.'

'The general says he cannot stop anything if an order is given,' Tjong said, 'but he will try as hard as he can to discourage overt military action, which is all we can expect. He is doubtful about covert action because there are many different military groups, and control of all of them is a little loose these days. And they don't have much money.'

'So I can tell my colleagues, for the umpteenth time, that we are unlikely to face a military threat from the south?'

'Unlikely, yes.' *But they may do other unfriendly things*, Tjong told himself.

The maid approached with a trolley and Tjong started to pour himself a brandy.

'Help yourselves, gentlemen,' he said.

'Sorry, we have to go now,' Dr Wong said. Adding, 'We appreciate your help in this matter, Mr Tjong. I can tell you that a more tangible thank you will be forthcoming later.' They were already getting into the car as Tjong proceeded to add ginger ale to his brandy. *'Tiew nia seng!'* he uttered his favourite obscenity.

His property holdings had been steadily losing their value, and they were now worth half what he had put in. Not to mention the steady slide in share prices. So much for faith. He would need to wait a long time to break even on his investments in Singapore. At the same time, his old friends in Indonesia had all fallen by the wayside. And Othman was becoming difficult. Even the generals were scared of him now, but they did not have the balls for a coup. ABRI's slide began when their man, Soeharto, overplayed his hand. He had bankrupted the country and muddied the water for everybody else.

'Tiew nia seng,' Tjong muttered as the visitors' car glided out of the driveway.

Their Merc had a special sticker which allowed them to go anywhere they wanted, while people like himself had to stay home. Singapore markets were closed, but there was a massacre on other markets.

'Tiew nia seng!'

But Johore held promise.

Dr Wong had sensed that Tjong's mood was changing. The man was known to rant and rave sometimes.

'What do you think?' he asked the contemplative Dr Rajah as the driver moved the car out into the almost empty road, heading for Orchard Road.

He hadn't said a word to Tjong. He had merely smiled on arrival, listened to the proceedings, then smiled as they got up to leave.

'He is angry, but I think it is nice to get confirmation from a civilian about the Jakarta business. His businesses have all been in trouble ever since his friend's fall from office, you know that.'

'Yes, but he had always kept his money here. I hear he is operating over there on overdrafts, based on physical assets, of course. So if they seize his assets, they will have to take his debts as well. Clever fellow,' said Dr Wong.

'Drop me off at the clinic. I've got my car there.'

His car, too, had a special sticker.

Dr Wong returned to the Blue Room. Only a few members had gone home as the long day wore on. He walked in to be told that the Great Man would be addressing members at 8 p.m., by which time it was expected that the new border would have achieved some permanency.

All day the line had been reinforced by men and armour and concrete barriers. There had been some exchange of gunfire, smothered by RSAF fighters. There was doubt and confusion in Kuala Lumpur, where longstanding strains in the ruling coalition had created political instability. The Malaysians, too, were intensely conscious of the presence of the *Truman*, which cast a fearful shadow over the entire region. Had the Singaporeans come to an arrangement with the Americans? How could they allow this sort of aggression? Things were afoot at the United Nations, but while they talked Singapore troops were digging in, and they were winning the propaganda war.

'It's all *kiasu* out there,' one member commented in the Blue Room.

Kiasu, failure or the appearance thereof, was worse than losing face.

Champagne had been brought in with the evening meal, which was a choice of six varieties of takeaway packets. The Great Man's speech might be telecast live, but there were concerns about its effect north of the border. Better not make too much noise, let the border settle. But there was this silent, malevolent thing that hung over the Blue Room, the fear that lurked in the darkest corners of pragmatic thinkers: race riots. That terrible thing that defied reason, the urge to run wild with whatever weapon one could lay one's hands on, raping, looting, killing, burning. The genie that could not be put back into the bottle until its bloody wrath had been appeased. *Amok* was a Malay word. But so far there was no news. All was quiet. Too quiet.

On Singapore's part, the faces that appeared on television to read those Important Statements had been mostly non-Chinese. The Mindef people working as links for the international media were also similarly mostly non-Chinese. Singapore had done all in its power to give the conflict a non-Chinese face. People of Indian, Sri Lankan and other origins had been corralled together with Eurasians to do their duty for the national cause. The transparency of the exercise raised a hoot in the HDB heartlands, the Housing Board's tower blocks where the majority of the population lived. But that was only to be expected; they were a shrewd people.

Bernama reported the first outbreak. A group of youths, pre-sumably Malays, had ransacked some shops in Batu Caves, an outlying KL suburb. There was no mention of casualties. A curfew had been in place in most towns and cities since midday, because of the aerial attacks.

As nightfall approached the entire population was jittery, for race riots are a double-edged sword, sometimes triple-edged. No one could be safe. The Chinese dragon would definitely rise to defend itself if attacked. How could you associate a Singapore military operation with the loyal Chinese who had lived peace-fully and with mutual respect with Malays and Indians all these years? Singapore troops manning new border crossings had been told to let in refugees – of any kind.

It was almost 8 p.m. and all members of the Blue Room were seated. The Great Man walked in with two assistants and two bodyguards. He was beaming from ear to ear. Spontaneous applause broke out and he stopped his progress to the podium to savour the moment and shake hands. His father would have been proud if he had been there, but the vagaries of politics had seen the old warrior swept away from the middle echelons in the PAP's peculiar hierarchical set-up.

Singapore is run like a prosperous business, and it seeks talent everywhere; in the clan associations, the chambers of commerce, in the constituency committees, family business networks, in the professions and the bureaucracy. Meritocracy demands it; but a meteoric rise to the top is on the condition of total devotion and loyalty to the men who represent the status quo. It helps, of course, if your father or uncle is a party heavy. But Steven Chong Yoke Lin was different. His party coup had been brilliant; a deep and damaging split had been avoided only when entrenched kingmakers finally accepted the reality that there had been a sea change in Singapore politics.

Steven Chong, hardly forty and without a Harvard or Oxford degree, just a polytechnic computer studies graduate, was indeed the Great Man that Singapore needed and had hankered after in the twilight of the authoritarianism that had afflicted the country for many years. Tonight, here in the Blue Room, this was his moment, the ultimate vindication of the trust that the people of Singapore had placed in him. The tallish man with a slight stoop, intense eyes and close-cropped, swept-back hair, was wearing the old PAP 'uniform' of white open-necked, short-sleeved shirt. The significance did not escape the chamber. He was trying to establish continuity with Singapore's troubled past and glorious future. The strains of *Majulah Singapura*, the national anthem, came over the speakers.

There was more applause. Then the Great Man spoke.

Chapter Three

'My fellow citizens,' Steven Chong began. 'We have today achieved the first of many momentous actions to create a great and prosperous country that will be the shining light of the new millennium. The story that began with a small trading post at the dawn of history has now achieved some of its promise.

'There is a way to go yet. It was Chinese genius that built this great city and what it stands for, the transcendental power of our culture and enterprise. The early immigrants had to work very hard to set the foundations, and their successors have not wasted their inheritance. Others, too, have come; for there were, and still are, many different byways and highways of migration. And we have been gracious and tolerant enough to find room for them. The unmitigated cruelty of the Japanese during the occupation years will never be forgotten, but there is no profit in revenge. There are things we can learn from the Japanese, and we must use all avenues in our march to a glorious future. But today the Singapore Lion roared. *Roared!*'

Roar! Roar! Roar!

Excitement crackled like static. The members got the drift, and made lion-like roaring noises.

Yes, it is going very well, Chong told himself, taking a dramatic pause for a sip of water.

'We have but seized only what we need to live. We need water. That's what this action is all about. I won't make the *lebensraum* claim, the old German cry for living space, although they did not really need any more and *we* desperately require more of. This is our destiny. It was pre-determined from the very beginning; our prosperity and our need for water were bound to seek out a secure solution.

'We can never hope to have sufficient storage facilities to withstand any prolonged water cut. And we have never accepted that we will allow this Damocles' Sword to hang over our heads indefinitely. Even if we were to start desalination projects on a massive basis to make us self-sufficient, there is no guarantee that the Malaysians will not find some other reason to show their disrespect of everything that Singapore stands for. A one billion dollar desalination plant will only meet ten per cent of our water requirements. We need four more to become somewhat self-sufficient, on present consumption levels. The infrastructure problems are too great for a small trading island like ours. Where are we going to find the land for them? The storage tanks have already taken some of our beautiful woodlands. We need more land to build factories and offices to generate the money for such expensive infrastructure works, while at the same time maintaining our standard and quality of life. It is a *real lebensraum* scenario.

'It was only a matter of time before the events of today would have occurred, but we would have been the victims and they the victors without this pre-emptive action on our part. This beautiful city that stands like a diamond in a sea of corruption, laziness, intolerance and envy would be reduced to an urban slum if we ignore the mounting levels of hatred across the Causeway. Our ancestors will all be smiling today. It is destiny.'

Roar! Roar! Roar!

'This brilliant military action has given us the opportunity to create a permanent environment for survival. We now have the land and water and the critical mass to call ourselves a nation. A parallel is Hong Kong with its New Territories. And if we approach Sabah and Sarawak with the offer of creating a new federation, there is no saying at this stage what the eventual make-up of South-East Asia will be like.

'You know there is strong antipathy in those two states against KL's long-distance rule. They don't get an equitable share of the revenue, and yet they are saddled with governors and heads of departments from KL, and the tragic loss of their jungle timber. These disaffected elements can be harnessed fruitfully. We had not acted so far because we needed the success of Operation Temasek to tempt them and dissuade KL from resisting too much.

'You will note that we have achieved our objective with minimal casualties. That is the key to achieving a peaceful resolution from this moment on. Military action is being scaled down rapidly, and the onus is on the Malaysians if they wish to extend the conflict. Their options are limited for a few days at least without air cover. That will allow the line of control to settle, and we are pouring enough concrete to provide that sense of permanence.

'Tomorrow will see a calm and peaceful start to a new dawn, in every sense of the word. I would like to remind our news editors that I don't want any jingoistic talk. They should highlight the new era of peace with the removal of irritants. From here on peace is the key. I shall, of course, be initiating talks. We will be working through the night. In the meantime, we remain quietly confident that success is ours.'

Roar! Roar! Roar!

The champagne was being opened when a message came up on the central screen, an edited version of the Bernama news agency report on an incident in Chow Kit Road in KL, an old flashpoint of racial disturbances in the Malaysian capital. Some shops were said to have been set on fire.

The fact that it was a Bernama report meant that the Malaysian government wanted it known. Naturally, the news had a dampening effect in the room, but aides continued to pour out the drinks, and Chong said, raising his glass, 'May the Singapore Lion roar long and loud!'

And they drank their toast to cries of 'Aye, aye' as if they were in Parliament.

The change in the mood of the assembly after the message about the Chow Kit Road incident became more noticeable as the conversation switched to civilian matters in KL; not that the incident was totally unexpected. Most members, of course, had been aware of the report for some time before it came up on the Blue Room screen. The consensus was that there would be no major race riots this time, for any attacks on the Chinese would provide the justification for Singapore's military action. And there had not been the time to whip up racial hatred; therefore, political forces beyond the control of the government must be at work.

That had its pros and cons. Malaysia at war with itself would be a weak enemy, but the Chinese segment of Malaysia's population would have a price to pay. Most people in Singapore had always had strong family connections with Malaysia. These people would have to be pacified; but first, the news would have to be played down, not blacked out.

'There is no way we can stop people tuning into Malaysian radio and television. The phones and the Internet will be running hot,' Steven Chong said. 'A blackout will only hurt our credibility. So how to douse these flames? Only the Malaysians can do that. We can, on the other hand, offer to open our borders to any Malaysians who wish to come south for protection. That has been the case since this afternoon. We are not looking for passports, just IDs will do.'

Chong was thinking aloud. He called his old friend Tan Chin Bock, retired and in poor health. Tan, who came from an old Straits Chinese family, seven or eight generations in Malacca, had impeccable contacts across the Causeway.

'Find out what is going on,' Chong told him.

Not that he really needed to, for Chong had his own network of party members and bureaucrats monitoring events and giving him constant updates.

Singapore had always discouraged its politicians and image makers from playing the race card. For years the multiracial message had been drummed into the population. That is not to say that matters Chinese were ignored. The PAP had always been aware of the make-up of its constituency, especially the Housing Board heartland, that vast multitude living in clusters of tall towers, the middle band of voters who decided the election result and who needed careful monitoring.

The pragmatic view was that no one would want to play the race card in Malaysia. All parties knew that, but then, there were extremists in every segment of the population. Singaporeans still remembered the racial bloodbath of the 60s. *Lest we forget*, the events of the time were highlighted in a multimedia exhibition, for there were new generations growing up relatively unaware of Singapore's bloody past.

The brief marriage with Malaysia had been a disaster. It had lasted only twenty-three months, and the acrimony of the parting had never been overcome. There was always something to upset sensibilities. But it was Singapore's founding Prime Minister and the then Senior Minister, Lee Kuan Yew, who had started the ball rolling in one of the more unnecessary episodes of name-calling by making derogatory remarks about Johore, and things had gone downhill from there.

Then there was the business with Indonesia's Habibie in the late 90s. Lee Kuan Yew had said, and he had made sure it was reported, that 'the market' would not take kindly to Dr Habibie's appointment as Vice-President. Then when Dr Habibie had finally become President, Singapore had been tardy in sending the usual congratulations. It had not escaped the canny doctor's notice as he read the goodwill messages from elsewhere.

After that little hurt had been overcome somewhat by a mixture of sweet words and gifts of food and medicine amidst Indonesia's financial difficulties during the regional economic meltdown, more bad news had started coming out of Indonesia. The gang rape of Chinese women, and the killings, looting and burning were bad enough, then had come word of the organised robbery of Chinese graves. The details had been gruesome; talk of bones being scattered, some relatives collecting the bones and cremating them, others reburying them. This had been a very painful development for a people that held their elderly in high regard and practised ancestor-worship.

There was now a growing consciousness in Singapore of a Chinese island in a Malay sea, 'a Chinese pimple on a Malay face', as some unkind people would say, a feeling resisted by the government that was aware of the dangers of a siege mentality. Singapore had to be regionalised, then globalised. Singaporeans should regard Jakarta or Kuala Lumpur, Manila or Bangkok, Penang or Phuket, no more than a suburb of Singapore. The global city wished to be inclusive, not exclusive.

*

Cohen had also seen the Bernama report, and Janet Lim gasped aloud when he told her. She knew what a race riot was. She had heard graphic reports of the notorious May 13 outbreak in the 60s. It had caught the population unprepared. When the clashes had settled into a stalemate of mutual terror, Malay soldiers had taken sides. That sort of total unpreparedness would not happen again, but if Malay troops took sides again it would be another story.

There were still people who remembered what it was like when Singapore's own small Malay community had suddenly erupted in a violent rampage in Geylang. Riot police had finally put it down, but in all that confusion one name had come to stand for the carnage: Syed Albar. A fiery speaker with the power to cast a hypnotic spell, he had been accused of haranguing and goading Malays to go on the warpath – an accusation strongly resisted but equally strongly levelled by Singapore leaders. Then there had been, for a time, an uneasy feeling in Singapore when Syed Jaafar Albar's son, Syed Hamid Albar, became Malaysia's Defence Minister, and later held other Cabinet portfolios.

Janet, with her ancestral roots in Penang, had been trying in vain to phone relatives all afternoon. She was in a state of panic when Cohen told her of the new disturbances. She remembered one of her aunts telling her that they had kept oil boiling on the stove to throw on their attackers as a last resort. Now this. The Malays were sure to look for Chinese scapegoats.

Janet was sick with fear. Her anguish was visible, and Cohen of the rampant libido backed off. He reached for the liquor cabinet and she knew that the moment had passed. She asked for a BGA, the old favourite – brandy ginger ale.

*

As night settled, Singapore switched on all its lights, a dramatic sight captured by satellites looking down on the diamond-shaped jewel a whisker north of the Equator. A bold statement of strength, or was it bravado? Singapore of the glistening glass and steel towers, the expressways with soaring flyovers flanked by lush greenery; museums and galleries and theatres; Singapore, with its extravagant shops, hotels and restaurants, was making a statement for all the world to see. Or was it a roar to hear? *We have arrived*, the Singapore Story was beginning to flower. An uneasy, steamy night. People beginning to pluck up the courage to go out into the city.

There were no visible signs of warfare, but most of the eating stalls and restaurants were closed. A crowd was beginning to gather in and around the Padang, the square of turf at the heart of the urban landscape. They were expecting their leaders to address them. The old joke was that the easiest way to knock out Singapore was to take out a few of its traffic lights, but that hadn't happened. In fact, nothing had happened to the city. The last Important Statement was that the military operation was over, sometime that evening, but there was still a feeling of unease among the population.

The television had continued showing the same boring old things. The reports and pictures from the front had that unidentifiable quality that suggested they could have come from anywhere. Mostly long-range photography and close-ups showing military vehicles parked somewhere. And plenty of jungle, which might as well be the back of McRitchie Reservoir for all anyone could say. There appeared to be a reluctance to show anything meaningful. How about Mersing, and Kota Tinggi and Keluang? Were they bluffing?

All along the people had only been kept informed through Important Statements, a tactic taken straight out of Stormin' Norman's book of warfare. The media was drip-fed, with just enough words and pictures to tell the story that Singapore wanted to be told; for Singapore did not wish to make things any worse for Malaysian leaders. Nothing more, no independent reporting, and Malaysia was following suit; they did not wish to broadcast a setback. The KL government's survival was at stake.

Telephones remained cut in many areas to keep the bad news from spreading. Radio, television and the newspapers had all been reined in, and they were reporting a uniform statement that there had been some military hostilities with Singapore and that the situation was quickly returning to normal. The people should remain calm while the government analysed the new developments. *Wayang kulit*, or shadow play, was in full flight, on both sides of the new border. Only the Internet bridged the information gap, but it had large holes.

★

Steven Chong became aware at about 10 p.m. that he had to address the people. A studio presentation might not be enough. He would have to make a public appearance to demonstrate confidence. And say what? He must not inflame the Malays by boasting of Singapore's military success. He should not be seen to be pouring oil on the communal flames in KL. He must play the whole thing down, and yet make sure the people understood that a Greater Singapore had been created, the old crossing points had been moved deep into Johore. The water supply was safe and, most importantly, there was nothing to fear. There was no military threat to the city.

He would appeal to the population to remain calm and not to embark on unseemly celebrations or merry-making. He hoped Singaporeans would understand the reasons. All that had happened was a slight redrawing of the map to secure Singapore's water supply, and in such an exercise there was no need to look for victory or defeat. He hoped the Malaysian leaders understood the situation. He would plead for a pragmatic approach; in other words, do not try to correct the situation.

He was making his way to the Padang when the first explosion went off. It was thought to have been a grenade, thrown at a pillar holding up a flyover on the PIE (Pan Island Expressway) to the airport; but the pillar had withstood the blast. The police had sealed the area and they were interviewing people house by house, flat by flat. Police and more soldiers were out on the street, a sight that the government had not wanted to present for the people to see.

Steven Chong cancelled his outing and decided to go back to the Blue Room, and gave instructions to police to tell the people to disperse quickly and go home.

There were three more grenade blasts, in the Tanjong Pagar area. A curfew would have to be reimposed quickly. Chong did not like the new development. Either the front line was leaking like a sieve, or these were home-grown traitors. They would have to be weeded out quickly, for the markets had to open on Monday. Failure to do so could do untold harm.

★

Cohen was glad that Janet was spending the night at his place. The embassy called to remind him that he should inform the embassy switchboard if he wished to leave the flat for any reason. Many foreigners were leaving on every available flight, for Changi International Airport had remained open throughout. Many in the diplomatic service and their dependents were also leaving. He was unclear if he himself would be in Singapore for long, but Janet was welcome to stay in his flat for as long as she wished. 'Thank God,' was all she said as she got dressed to go back to her flat to fetch some of her things; but she found police at the entrance who told her to go back inside and stay there until they received further instructions. She just managed a glimpse of the empty street.

★

Very quickly the iron curtain around Singapore and the new territory was strengthened even further. The soft underbelly, the southern waters adjacent to international shipping lanes, was sealed off by a mix of naval vessels, police patrol boats, reconnaissance aircraft and the six prized subs. But ships still had to come into the harbour and be allowed to leave without hindrance. Security within Harbour Board limits was beefed up with all shore leave cancelled.

The last time Fortress Singapore had fallen was because all its British guns faced seaward to the south. The guns had stayed useless and silent because the Japanese army had come from the north, marching down along the peninsula. An old story, but the lesson had been well learned; but Singapore had also realised quite early that it would have to surrender long before any fighting occurred on the island itself. It was indefensible. The war would have to be fought and won or lost elsewhere. Therefore, to draw the fighting away from itself, the coast to coast Mersing line, the extent of Singapore's territory, had been strengthened. Only the Malaysian army remained that could possibly take the war any further.

The RMAF stayed grounded as work continued to fill in the craters, and each time it looked as though the planes would be able to take off, the RSAF would return and undo all the good work, and the Malaysians were as yet unable to deploy their anti-aircraft missiles. They remained in the ordnance depots. Without air cover the navy stayed well clear of the action. So it would have to be a full ground attack, a risky venture, again, without air cover.

*

As dawn broke the following day, Saturday, Suleiman Bakri decided to telephone Jakarta. The Malaysian Prime Minister wished to speak to the President about an urgent matter. Colonel Othman Suprianto's accession to power in a military coup had some similarities to Suleiman's own master stroke, except that in Suleiman's case the young, ambitious lawyer had employed a political ambush of his bumbling Prime Minister. Suleiman was a relative outsider in the Umno (United Malay National Organisation) power structure, but in one fell swoop during a period of economic stagnation he and a small coterie of Kelantan Malays had outflanked the incumbents. It had been a shock to the system, but the people had not been particularly sad to see the old clique go. They had run out of ideas to save the economy, merely waging a fruitless word war with foreign speculators and twiddling with currency regulations. Suleiman looked on Othman as an usurper in the tradition of Soeharto, whereas in Othman's eyes Suleiman's arrival had lacked the validity of approved succession. Still, the two men were on speaking terms, without the effusive camaraderie of a Mahathir and Soeharto.

Chapter Four

There is a small museum at the headquarters of Kostrad, Indonesia's Army Strategic Reserve, in Jalan Pejambon, Jakarta. Inscribed on its marble walls are the names of every Kostrad soldier who had died in action in Indonesia's three foreign operations. It lost thirty-nine in Operation Trikora, the campaign to 'liberate' West New Guinea; 483 died in Operation Seroja to seize East Timor; and forty-six died in Operation Dwikora, the 'Crush Malaysia' campaign that was Sukarno's Confrontation. The last figure is generally believed to be a gross underestimation. Malaysians joke about the then Malaysian Prime Minister, Tunku Abdul Rahman, saying that he would fight Indonesia to the last drop of British blood. It was believable. In the event, Britain's decolonisation programme led to the creation of the Malaysian Federation together with Sabah and Sarawak, across the water in Borneo, and the ill-starred incorporation of Singapore.

Most of Sukarno's generals of the time have departed the scene, but ABRI, the Indonesian Armed Forces command structure, has a long memory, and when the generals met in President Othman's office in answer to an urgent summons, there was some glee at Malaysia's predicament. And no inclination to lose Indonesian lives for the benefit of either Malaysia or Singapore. They had anticipated Suleiman Bakri's approach, so when Othman was satisfied that his key generals and cabinet colleagues were present, he told his aide to put Suleiman on the line.

'*Selamat Pagi*, Tuan President.'

'*Selamat Pagi*, Tuan Perdana Mentri.'

Then Suleiman switched to English, for he was aware that, although both spoke Bahasa, they had difficulty understanding each other because of regional peculiarities of pronunciation. Othman's guttural Sulawesi patois could not be further from Suleiman's singsong Kelantanese.

'You know what has happened, but, *Insha Allah*, we will drive them back across the water,' said Suleiman.

'*Insha Allah*,' replied Othman.

'But we need a little help. You know our planes have been grounded. They have not been destroyed, just put out of action because of damage to the runways.'

'Yes, I believe so,' said Othman.

'I am suggesting that we put up a united front, sort of, suggest to the Singaporeans that Indonesian forces, including your planes, might come into play unless this matter is returned to the status quo,' said Suleiman.

'Why?'

'Because, Tuan President, we have to stop the Chinese here and now, otherwise you are looking at a Chinese empire right in the centre of our world. Make no mistake, this is a Chinese Singapore, and they think in terms of centuries. They might even take Indonesian territory under the pretext of providing a refuge for your Chinese citizens,' answered Suleiman.

'Are we not stretching the point a bit? You must realise that you have brought this on yourself. You must have known that as long as you talked tough about supplying water, Singapore was bound to do something about it themselves, rather that wait for someone to come to their aid. No one has, as far as I am aware.'

'You are right, Tuan President, but you must be aware of the presence of the American carrier *Truman* in these waters. We are beginning to suspect an American role.'

'The more reason for us to be circumspect. Do you know what that thing can do?' asked Othman.

'We are getting the United Nations involved, *Insha Allah*. But China's veto in the Security Council might be a stumbling block,' offered Suleiman.

'Have you spoken to the Americans?'

'No. Actually, yes, and they had said the *Truman* just happened to be there; they were watching the situation.'

'You better talk to them and see what they have to say,' suggested Othman.

Othman had resisted referring to the often mentioned Five-Power Defence Arrangement banding together Britain, Australia and New Zealand, together with Malaysia and Singapore, as a defence umbrella for the newly independent British territories in South-East Asia. Sadly, the FPDA had lost its teeth after Malaysia's interest cooled and the Arrangement had been scaled down into a defence consultative body in 1998; but Australia continued to send its fighter aircraft on rotation to Butterworth, an air base on the Malaysian mainland facing Penang. Whatever its shape or form, the FPDA's birth had followed Indonesia's Confrontation, and the Arrangement's main but unnamed target had always been Indonesia.

Othman could not hold back any longer and he pushed the blade in, although he was aware that the FPDA, despite still being intact and pretending to be active, was in reality in a state of disarray; the exquisite irony of it all excited him.

'I suppose the Five-Power thing will be unable to do anything for you.'

Ouch. That hurt.

'No, I don't think so,' replied Suleiman.

'Why?' asked Othman, as if he didn't know.

'Singapore told the others to stay out of it. That we will solve our own problems this time.'

'Oh,' Othman paused, then said, 'my response to you is that you should give us time to consider the situation. I am sorry, but that has to be my answer to you at present. Maybe the problem will be solved some other way, *Insha Allah*.'

'Er, yes, yes. Thank you, Tuan President.'

'*Selamat Pagi*, Tuan Perdana Mentri.'

'*Selamat Pagi*.'

And, as an aside, Othman told his generals: 'As the Chinese say, a curse on both their houses!'

*

Suleiman Bakri paused a moment to admire the bougainvillaea bursting in myriad formations and colours outside his window, then turned to his officials and wondered aloud whether he had misread the Indonesian President's mind. For it was one of his predecessors, Dr Habibie, who, in a public display of irritation at not being congratulated by the Singapore Government on his becoming President, had swept his arm across a map of South-East Asia and said: 'Look at the map. All the green is Indonesia. And that red dot is Singapore. Look at that!'

Well, that red dot has grown into a large pool of blood, Suleiman told himself. *We would have to do the cleaning up the hard way.*

The irony was that there were three squadrons of Australian fighter-bombers at the base in Butterworth – two squadrons of F-18s and one of the ageing Mirages. They all stayed grounded, although Butterworth's runways had been left untouched by Singapore aircraft.

There were more racial disturbances, the last thing that Suleiman wanted. They were reported in several small towns, but fortunately they were minor incidents. The situation in south Johore was that the Singaporeans were strengthening their grip and that the population had been cowed into silence. Something like 300,000 Malaysians had come under Singapore rule, a full ten per cent of the island's present population. The curfew in the occupied area had been lifted for a couple of hours in the morning for people to stock up on groceries, but the markets had remained closed. Suleiman had learned that all police and armed forces personnel discovered behind the lines had been disarmed and allowed to go free, but some had been taken away to detention in Singapore. He could guess, but he could not be sure, if Singapore had its stooges in Johore. This man Jaffar Ibrahim had been seen scurrying about Johore Bahru. He had been seen going to the palace. The Sultan had a satellite phone, but it remained unused and unanswered. Had they taken it from him? Suleiman still had a few people with satellite phones to get some information out of the occupied area. But he, in turn, had nothing to tell them except to remain calm.

There had been a Cabinet session and two meetings of the quickly convened Operations Room, a relic from the Emergency of the 50s and 60s when communist insurgents had tried to seize the country in an extravagant onslaught on colonialism. The discussions had been inconclusive, apart from decisions to protest, seek the support of friendly countries, try and get the UN involved, and call for calm.

Suleiman had to overrule a general's half-hearted suggestion to launch an immediate offensive. Not without air cover, he had said.

Suleiman Bakri could not put his finger on it, but he had a vague feeling there was something of a reluctance among Ops Room members to come forward with workable suggestions to rid the land of the invaders. Had the political turmoil of the recent past infected the armed forces? Such a development had traditionally been considered unlikely, for Malaysia's military leaders had always managed to insulate themselves from politics; still, the sad result of these endless discussions was that no concrete plan of action emerged.

The truth of the situation was that the armed forces chiefs were furious at the politicians who had taken some particularly incomprehensible decisions. The army had been undergoing the painful shift from counter-insurgency to a more general framework when the defence budget had suffered successive reductions, which had also led to reductions in maintenance schedules, training and joint exercises. The politicians who decided to buy F-18s from the United States, Hawk 200s from Britain and MiG-29s from the old Soviet Union had left the RMAF saddled with three totally incompatible streams of maintenance and spare parts, too much for the limited resources available. Some years before, Professor Paul Dibb, head of the Strategic Studies Centre at the Australian National University in Canberra, had said that in South-East Asia, apart from Singapore, military maintenance was quite deficient and that he doubted that many planes or warships could operate in a crisis for more than a few days. Costly weaponry had not translated into competent military organisations in Asian countries, again excluding Singapore. And, at around the same time, a US Army War College assessment had said that the SAF (Singapore Armed Forces) remained the strongest military force in the region. Malaysia's generals were aware of these assessments, but they had to live with the limitations of the political situation, dominated by Suleiman Bakri's shaky hold on power.

★

Ismail Sebi, the Action Man of the Internal Security Department, had been strangely silent throughout the discussions in the Ops Room, just listening; but he knew he could launch a bombing campaign in Singapore at short notice. He had the people and their requirements on site. The thing had cost a bit of money, but he was convinced that he had to prepare for a situation such as this, for he had been among the first to warn the Cabinet many years ago of the possibility of a Singapore invasion, a suggestion ridiculed as being completely over the top. So he sat back and watched the other members of the Operations Room squirm. Some generals kept pushing for an immediate land offensive, with or without air cover. *Were they serious?* Heavy casualties were inevitable and unacceptable. The runways at the two RMAF bases now had missile protection, but the officers were inexperienced, and launchers were also coming under air attack, keeping repair crews away. As things stood, the action remained around the two air force bases, while the rest of the country remained unscathed. Still, Malaysian forces had suffered forty-eight dead and over sixty wounded, eighteen seriously.

Suleiman Bakri believed that the war had to be taken to the Singaporeans, and that depended on control of the air. The Singaporeans were trying to maintain a level of normalcy by keeping their harbour and Changi Airport open as if nothing was wrong. That should not be allowed to continue; they had to know some pain.

His thoughts were wandering to such esoteric topics as trying to get a Big Bomb from the Pakistanis when Ismail Sebi whispered something in his ear which brought a rare smile to his lips. The greying police officer left the room quickly; he knew Suleiman would get full support in the Operations Room for what he was about to do. He went back to his office and called in four men from one of his more obscure sections. The phones were running hot again with long forgotten code words.

There had been eight grenade attacks on cars parked in housing estates around Singapore. Soldiers had shot dead two men who were seen running away. A grenade had been thrown at a perimeter fence of Changi International Airport, sparking the stationing of sentries at ten metre intervals. You could see the mass of uniformed men from the road leading up to the airport, a fearful sight for travellers, but still they streamed in in an unbroken line, taking any flight out of Singapore. Taxis with special stickers had been made available to take these people to the airport during curfew hours.

Another Important Statement on television said financial markets would open as usual on Monday; so too all offices, schools and colleges. There was nothing to fear as the culprits had been caught and troublemakers should not be allowed to spread alarm – double-speak for Singaporeans who took it to mean that things could get real bad.

In Chinatown especially they feared the worst, but they were prepared, for they were all aware of their precarious grip on the map of South-East Asia. They would not go down without a fight. Their young men were already bearing arms, for the national service call-up had been going on continuously for two days. The island, its waters, and the new areas on the peninsula were all crawling with men in jungle-green. Reservists up to the age of forty had also been called up. Singapore was now sealed tight; the more mature men given the guard and surveillance duties. The reservoirs, all the water pipes, power grids, gasworks, the harbour, Sentosa and the outlying islands, every possible weakness had been considered. And still a grenade went off in Fullerton Square.

*

About 4 a.m. on Sunday the Blue Room was called into session to consider once again whether the curfew should be lifted for the markets and schools to open as promised, for there was now the real danger that terrorists would be able to move about freely. Explosions near the city centre were unthinkable for the trauma they would cause. People were not sleeping despite the late hour, for word about the explosions was spreading as fast as the Internet could carry the traffic. If the curfew continued and the markets failed to open, it would be a body blow for a financial centre like Singapore. For better or worse, the markets had to open.

Steven Chong was worried. The boyish face on the bullet head was now set in a permanent scowl. He could order his planes to give Kuala Lumpur a taste of what their terrorists were doing to his city. The Blue Room would overrule him on the suggestion, he knew, but he couldn't help wondering whether that would not produce an instant result, bringing calm and quiet to Singapore and its markets. Well, he need not tell his colleagues *everything*…

He called Dr Wong out of the chamber and they went into a secretarial annexe. What did he think of the proposal that a single F-16 drop two bombs, one on a roundabout in Ampang Road and one in the centre of Putra Jaya, the administrative centre where most of the government offices and Ministries were located, just to remind KL that two could play the game?

'That is a dangerous game,' Dr Wong told him.

'I know, but on the other hand the gamble might succeed. They might be persuaded to call off their campaign within Singapore,' said Chong.

'I doubt it. Pushed to the wall, the Malays will fight as well as anybody. They are unlikely to yield,' said Dr Wong.

'We have to do something, and quickly. We have hardly an hour to daybreak.'

'Yes, Steven. I am aware of that. What we should do is to be more vigilant. We must fight these terrorists at street level.' The good doctor was allowed to call the Prime Minister by his first name in private.

'So we sail the same course?' asked Chong.

'Yes, and tell the navy to expect infiltration attempts by sampans, and that the land wall must be leak-proof.'

'Right, so the markets and schools and colleges will open as usual.'

The Prime Minister walked into the Blue Room to suggest this course of action and the council concurred.

★

Asma Latiff was one of Malaysia's secret weapons – a cliché, but true. The attractive woman in her early forties had married a Singaporean and obtained Singapore citizenship; she carried a Singapore passport and identity card. The divorcee from Kota

Bahru, in the far north-east corner of the Malaysian peninsula, had come a long way, thanks to a kindly man from KL who had offered the struggling young woman a deal too good to refuse. He had offered to find her a good man to marry; she would follow him to Singapore and start a new life. She would receive unspecified training before she went, and one day, perhaps, she might be able to do her benefactors a favour. She was the ace in Ismail Sebi's pack, for she had turned out to be an extremely intelligent and brave woman.

She learned about chemicals and fuses, grenades and rockets, and to stay well away from all matters political. The lessons had not been easy, for she had also needed to go to English language classes. And she had needed lessons in dressing, make-up and skin care, and she had to learn to walk gracefully in high heels. The result had been pleasing; anyone would want to marry the new Asma, and matters had progressed satisfactorily.

Ismail Sebi decided to play his ace at the first opportunity, but he would try not to sacrifice his people. They would be given every assistance to save themselves. But Chong and company would have plenty to think about. Curfew again? Close the markets? Where's the next one going to be? There was no need for Ismail Sebi to tell his Prime Minister about Asma, and others like her, that he had in place in Singapore. It was just one of those things that people in his peculiar business did, and not many people needed to know. If anything happened to him, they would have to look into the files in his safe at the ministry to discover the secret of Asma Latiff and the others.

All day Asma had been dreading the call, ever since she heard about the Important Statements on the television, for she was not watching the box at the time and it was a neighbour who had shouted over to her. She had turned on the television and the message was repeated in other languages, including Malay.

She called her assistant, Mohammed Ariff, established in the flat below hers in Geylang, to alert him to the possibility of a call to action. The best part was that her husband was a policeman and not expected to be able to come home for at least twenty-four hours. Mohammed Ariff's old mother came over to babysit her two young children, giving her a free hand to do her work. Of course, the old woman did not have to know what that work was, except that it was important and that it was 'for the government'.

She had another assistant, Ah Ching, a bitter young student related to a man who had been detained for almost two decades under Singapore's draconian Internal Security Act. The government had accused the man of being a communist, and had offered to release him if he signed a confession. He had angrily denied that he was ever a communist, and had refused to sign anything. And although the Internal Security Department had come to believe that they might have made a mistake, it was too much of a loss of face to concede the point. So the man stayed inside, and the detention order had been renewed year after year as a matter of course. The humanity had gone out of the department long ago, just the casual cruelty of an overblown ego remained. The man's family had given up all efforts to try and secure his release, for the government would not budge. The man had to admit his mistake. He would not. So he stayed inside.

The bloody-mindedness of the Singapore government in these matters was well-known and well-publicised. The pursuit of opposition politicians in the courts and the PAP's habitual legal victories had given PAP politicians an aura of invincibility. In addition, Singapore's economy, even at its darkest hour, was still the best in all Asia. The island state was the best managed in all its many facets. The first fully wired city of the cyber age. Even in the performing arts; music, drama and art in all media found the government a benevolent source of assistance. But, of course, organisers of all stage productions and public meetings and shows must still get a police licence. One of the annoyances of life that Singaporeans had come to accept as part of the price of their prosperity. Guided democracy of sorts. But underneath the facade of a quiescent population a streak of rebellion born of the helplessness of the individual bubbled on. All under surveillance, of course, but, as always, parts of it unseen and unsuspected.

*

Ah Ching, who had escaped national service and the call-up because of his bad lungs, lived in Chinatown and therefore could not move about as freely as Asma and Mohammed Ariff could at the far end of Geylang. He had to wait for the curfew to be lifted. Asma called from a public phone to tell him that he should not do anything to attract attention and that he was to wait for the curfew to be lifted. Now all three were on the alert. They knew what they might have to do. And finally, at about 5 a.m., the phone rang for Asma. It was Ismail Sebi, from the other time, other place. He wanted a favour…

★

Dom Thomas, too, was waiting for the curfew to be lifted so he could move to his cousin's place after spending the night at Tessy's flat in Tiong Bahru, which was the closest to Fatso's when a day of rising tensions had led to the first of the Important Statements. And some night it had turned out to be. They had set out to go to town some time during the night only to be told by police to go home quickly and stay there. So they had been listening to the Moody Blues, keeping an eye on the television for Important Statements, and talking about the good times.

Tessy's wife, Rose, had gone to bed about 3 a.m. but the two old friends stayed up with a bottle of scotch and good cheer. The sense of something awful about to happen failed to dent their spirits. It was like old times, except that then it used to be in some bar around Bras Basah Road.

'Whatever happened to Peng Ah Pat? Remember the small guy who was always hanging out at the *wayangs*?'

'They say he finally settled down five or six years ago, for the sixth or seventh time. With a girl half his age.'

Well, in Peng's case, it was really not divorce and remarriage. Moving out of one relationship and moving into another without too much paperwork was his way. But each time he would buy new furniture and fridge and television and stereo and everything else to set-up house. And leave it all behind when he moved on. A costly business for a man of his limited means as a lawyer's clerk. Quite a guy; they say he'd chased every new heroine on the Chinese opera scene most of his adult life. He couldn't help it. It was always instant love. He was always checking out the *wayangs* all over the island. The *wayang* represented theatre for the masses in those days, and he loved it. The *doom-doom-cha* drums and clashing cymbals, the screeching performers in garish make-up, the jumping and twisting in the unsteady spotlights, while all the time the night-market audience went about their business of haggling, buying and eating, only some actually sitting down on the wooden stackables to watch the *wayang*.

Peng's day job was a pastime, his real calling was as a stage-door johnny. In between his nightly journeys he would drop into the Bras Basah bars to spend some time with his friends. Always broke, of course, for he spent all his spare cash on the *wayang* girls, past and future lovers. Flowers, small gold ornaments, transistor radios.

Then there was Raymond Choo, universally known as Randy, a name which described the accountant perfectly. He seemed to have withstood the government's puritanical attitude in these matters, for he had risen to a senior position in the civil service; now retired and passing the time as a company director. He was always with Wally the Quiet, so named because he never had anything to say but was always a part of the action, which, of course, was mostly drinking and eating out. Walter, too, had retired, but his health had failed and he was mostly housebound. There was no trace of Ching Quee, the one they called Oily because he weaved in and out of business and government seamlessly, accumulating great wealth.

Rahmat Majid was living the good life, with his third wife. He had pulled off the neatest con anyone could think of. The company he was working for at the time had handed out a contract for a $250 million building extension. While the work was in progress he approached the contractor and intimated to him that there was a ten per cent kickback involved, and, well, everyone on his side was getting a little anxious that the money had not been forthcoming.

After much to-ing and fro-ing, and with Rahmat making site inspections accompanied by the MD and the company chairman, the contractor became convinced of the need to pay. He made adjustments to the building to extract the ten per cent, and the money was paid into Rahmat's account in a bank in Australia.

Three weeks later Rahmat left the company, but it was another two months before the company became aware of why Rahmat had made such a hasty departure. The money could not be recovered and a police case was considered embarrassing, and the matter was allowed to be forgotten. And thus Rahmat made a clean getaway with $25 million.

'Call him, Dom,' Tessy said. 'He will want to show off. Why don't you go and have a good time?'

'Yes, I might, depending on how this thing settles down. Any idea where Larry is?'

'Ah yes, your big friend Larry Lim, the cigarette salesman. He gave up working some years ago after he married a rich widow. But it's a sad story.'

'How come?' asked Dom.

'Do you remember that he had this thing for fat women? A plump woman giggling is his idea of the height of erotic arousal. That's how he came to woo and marry his present wife. And they were happy together, until about ten years ago when he went to a wedding and there was this woman MC, a round, jolly woman called Lingling. She was, and is, everything that Larry loves in a woman. Fat and full of fun, but half his age, happily married, and not interested in his overtures. But he still can't stay away. A couple of years ago he went to a show where Lingling came on in shorts, rolled about the stage and asked her audience, "So you are happy seeing a little piggy dance, huh?" It was too much for Larry. He had difficulty breathing and he had to spend a couple of days in hospital. Poor guy. He still has a fixation on that woman.'

The bottle of scotch was almost empty, and Tessy was beginning to nod off. At 5 a.m. the pretty face of Norma Fonseca came on the television with the Important Statement that the curfew would be lifted at 2 p.m. and reimposed at 6 p.m. so that people who wished to perform their religious duties could do so. Dom took the sofa, and Tessy snored on the carpet with a cushion under his head.

Asma Latiff, Mohammed Ariff and Ah Ching had many things to do in those four hours.

Chapter Five

At the same time as two officers from the *Truman* were having a curry lunch at the American embassy that Sunday, Steven Chong, accompanied by Dr Wong and a few others, was having *nyonya laksa* at the *istana*, and people all over the island were getting ready to dash out the door at the stroke of two. Cooped up in flats, the claustrophobia was a palpable thing. Apart from the fear of death and injury in a military attack or a terrorist grenade blast, people were irritable and there had been fights and plenty of insults and obscenities flung across balconies and corridors over noisy televisions and the crack-crack of mahjong.

Tessy wanted to go to the Novenas, something he hadn't done in years, and so they set course for the church. They parked the car about a kilometre away when they saw the crowd in the distance. The roadsides were choked with people carrying lit candles in the bright sunlight, all standing still, unable to move forward. Dom and Tessy could hear the tinkle of altar bells and a faint chant, taken up quickly by the crowd even at this distance.

Hail Mary, full of grace…

The ancient chant rose to the heavens in waves that rolled from one end of the road to the other. Now the candles were being fixed on the cement pavement, and rosaries, some not having been used for years, were coming out of handbags. The traffic slowed to a crawl as the roadsides swelled with humanity, and still the crowd grew further down the road. The peculiar nature of the Singaporean that would not go overboard for any religion but who could believe in Buddha and Shiva, Confucius and Jesus all at the same time, created an acute and immediate need to pray for divine protection for loved ones at the front and comfort for the worried ones left behind. All over the island, joss sticks and paper money by the fistfuls wafted to the heavens their own supplications. All the temples, like the Hindu Sri Mariamman Temple and the Taoist-Buddhist Temple of

Heavenly Happiness (the Thian Hock Keng), and Sikh gurud-waras were open. So, too, was the golden-domed Sultan Mosque in the Muslim quarter, but there were few worshippers here; a heavy police presence kept most people away. Elsewhere the air was filled with mantras, chants and prayers in myriad languages, creating an aura of dread.

Steven Chong sensed the mood even before it was brought to his attention, but it was too late to change the curfew hours. Let the opiate of the masses do its work, for all the good it was going to do them. He was, of course, quoting Mao. Chong believed only in his own cerebral capabilities. The adventure still had some distance to go.

Driving on to the city, Tessy parked his car in a lane off South Bridge Road and they walked towards the Anglican cathedral. They could already hear *How Great Thou Art* in the distance, and as they dodged past growing numbers of people they could hear the low murmur of prayer, a louder hum of *Our Father Who art in heaven*… And they were still not even in the grounds of St Andrews. Something like ten thousand or twenty thousand people thronged the old cathedral, the grounds and surrounding roads. Tessy and Dom could not move forward any more, for the crowd would not yield. Then they heard the cracking voice of the old archdeacon intone the Grace, ringing out in the silence, *The peace of God that passeth all understanding*…

The *Amen* took a while to do the rounds, and then silence descended on the huge congregation. The peace of God, war of the races, or fear of the morrow? The crowd paused, unsure of what to do next, everyone intensely conscious of the young men who had taken up their guns and gone across the Causeway. In that moment of blessed silence, one clear voice cut through the gloaming. It was Christina Ong, near the north gate.

Abide with me, fast falls the even tide…

And the words tumbled out in a spreading ripple.

The darkness deepens, Lord with me abide…

Dom could see even Tessy, the old agnostic, mouthing the words.

With Christina Ong were four women from her fledgling Serangoon Garden A Cappella Singers. They waited a moment for the power of the hymn to sink in, then seamlessly, one by one, the five women started again. Christina began *Amazing Grace*, one joined her in *How sweet the sound*, another came in with the next line and soon all five were in perfect harmony, enveloping the crowd in a cocoon of beautiful sound that soothed the soul. The people stayed rooted to the ground, as if hypnotised. Christina and her group ran out of time, or she would have tried out some of their American spirituals. Another time, she told herself. But not like this!

★

Frail old Eleanor Prentice could not plough through the crowd to reach the cathedral; she only made it as far as High Street. She stood at a shop front, her granddaughter Mavis holding her tight so she would not crumple to the ground with the emotion that seized her. Eleanor sobbed quietly into Mavis' sleeve as they waited for Mavis' husband to try and bring the car to them. Her great-grandson, Simon, had gone off to the wars, somewhere in Johore.

'You know, my dear, the last time I sang *Abide With Me* like this was a long, long time ago. In Jalan Abdullah, in KL. The Japanese were coming and many families were leaving. One of our neighbours was an Indian family. He was a newspaper editor. Several of us met at the house and I remember singing it. And we also sang the goodbye song of the time. Vera Lynn's song.' And Eleanor mouthed the words, hardly a whisper.

Wish me luck, as you wave me goodbye,
Cheerio, here I go, on my way...

'Let us go home, Nan. We will talk later. Don't get upset. Everything will be all right.'

'That's what your grandfather said at the time, in Jalan Abdullah. We went to Australia, he was to follow us three months later. He never came home.'

'It was not his fault, Nan,' Mavis said defensively. 'His ship got torpedoed.'

'He should have come with us.'

Mavis was surprised at the edge in her grandmother's voice.

Something that happened such a long time ago was finding a resonance. The Japanese invasion had begun shortly after Eleanor, seven months pregnant with Mavis's mother Sophie, had reached Sydney, and Allied forces in Singapore surrendered to the Japanese on 15 February, 1942. The brutal Changi Prison and the deadly Burma Railway awaited the surviving troops, matched by equally brutal treatment of the civilian population.

But what did this gleaming metropolis have to do with those other dark times, other places? A city to match the spirit of the new millennium, with the gumption to get up and at 'em. Singapore had the most powerful air force in the region, subs and frigates to protect its waters, and a huge revolving army of national servicemen that could be marshalled and thrown into action quickly. Mavis' friend at work had told her that before long Singapore would be in a position to guarantee the safety and security of South-East Asia in its own right, with only a token contribution by the Americans. Mavis' friend should know. The friend's husband worked in the Prime Minister's Office.

★

All the while, the national service call-up and deployment continued without a break. Almost every family had a young man out there, or being prepared to be sent out. A husband, brother, father, uncle or cousin. The Mersing Line was being strengthened, the shores sealed with men and armour.

The forward bulwark was held out as the logical focal point for a Malaysian attack. And the air force was ready to blunt any offensive. The trucks had been rolling non-stop, earth-moving machines cleared and levelled ribbons of land which would serve as the killing fields if any attack came.

The mood in the Blue Room was that a Malaysian counter-attack might not be in the offing, but their focus had to be turned to something else. Moving the action to the United Nations would be a good idea. Efforts were already under way to persuade friendly countries to lean on the Malaysians to respect Singapore's legitimate aspirations to control its water supply. Water had to be the operative word in all discussions.

Captain Tan Howe Liang was leading a re-configured platoon of twelve, eight national servicemen and four full-timers. He and his number two, a sergeant, and two soldiers were full-timers. One of them had a video camera, telephone and laptop with satellite hooks. They had a rocket launcher, two mortars and three heavy machine-guns, plus grenades, regulation SAR-21s and side arms, plenty of food, and a regular run of supply trucks moving along the lines. More trucks continued to pour concrete, with more men building barriers. There were also the generals and regimental officers doing the rounds.

'If only they would leave us alone. We're being inspected to death,' the captain told his men.

He was about six kilometres west of Keluang; he could see the platoons immediately to the left and right, only about fifty metres away. That was how closely strung the line was. In time the gaps between them would be filled again, making an unbroken line of men and barriers, shore to shore. But there had been little action; the Malaysians appeared not to have reacted. Had the air force been that effective in keeping them at bay?

There was an unfortunate incident early in the morning, some distance to the west. One of the Singapore platoons thought they saw movement in a rubber estate on the other side and sent out four men to check what it was. To their surprise, they discovered that it was a group of people taking evasive action, ducking and weaving behind the trees, and the Singaporeans suspected the worst. They were well ahead of their lines, they became jittery, but they finally circled round and cornered the other group, and thirty seconds of gunfire ended their running and dodging. Five rubber tappers, three men and two women, lay dead. A mixed group of Chinese, Malays and Indians.

Three platoons sent men forward to bring back the bodies. One of those things, Captain Tan told his sergeant. The men needed time to gain confidence. They had to face battle to stop being so jittery. Malaysia's substantial reply to the incursion was being put together even as they spoke, he was sure. He hoped his men would not become careless just because nothing was happening. The only casualties among Singaporean forces thus far were due to accidents; two when a jeep overturned, one when a gun went off accidentally, and another when a tree fell on an NS man.

It had rained twice, each time a burst that lasted about two hours. From his position Captain Tan could see down to gently sloping valleys to east and west, for he was at the edge of the central spine of the peninsula. There were the geometrical shapes of rubber and oil palm plantations and swathes of jungle, already cleared of their big timber. Probably stolen by illegal loggers. He could see one angry red patch of land that had been cleared of all its vegetation, for oil palm most probably. Maybe a new township with its regulation computer chip factory. The jungle would eventually vanish in these parts. Wisps of cotton wool cloud drifted from the South China Sea; they would coalesce into showers during the night. He was thankful for the bug spray and mosquito nets. Sleep would be impossible otherwise. There was always a mosquito buzz in his ear, in spite of the repellent on his uniform, around the collars and sleeves.

He opened a bar of chocolate and broke off half for his number two.

'What do you think, Silva? You think they'll attack tonight?'

'We'll be ready,' the sergeant replied. 'There will always be three men on sentry duty. Three on, three off. We won't be taken by surprise.'

'Yes, I know. And we have the warning system.'

'Are the Americans helping us with that?' asked Silva.

'We don't need them. We have our own ways. And, Sergeant, don't hesitate to call me, however unimportant you may think it might be. I'm not here for a holiday,' said Tan.

A jeep rumbled up, and there was a two-star general in it. Or was it three stars? It was too dark to tell. Captain Tan didn't immediately recognise the general, but he saluted and stood to attention.

'At ease, young man,' Brigadier General Soh Huck Cheng said.

He would be on the road all night, going up and down the line checking everything himself. His adjutant, a sleepy captain, was going to be sick of him. And the driver complained that the jeep was making a fearful noise, drawing attention to itself. The general would be a sitting duck if the Malaysians were watching.

'Haven't I seen you somewhere?' the General asked, and Captain Tan remembered that crooked smile and broken nose.

'The anniversary party at Toa Payoh last month, sir. You gave me the medal in the sharpshooting section.'

'Good, good. Keep it up. Is everything all right? Do you need anything?' asked the General.

'Everything is A-OK, sir. We are ready for anything.'

'You mean, you don't want some chicken rice or something?' The general laughed.

'I'll be on my way.'

And he was gone in a rumble of engine revs and rasping exhaust.

★

Ambassador Johnson telephoned Steven Chong some time during the evening to convey the gist of a conversation he had had with the Secretary of State.

'The question he asked was simple, and you will understand that the Secretary is being briefed on developments,' Johnson told the Prime Minister.

'Yes, yes. So what did he say?'

'The Secretary asked me, and I quote, "How long do you think the tail will wag the dog?" You know the implication? He doesn't think you can hold the position for long.'

'Well, we can. Otherwise we would not have embarked on this line of action. Of course, so long as your government continues its even-handed approach,' said Chong.

'Of course, we are not taking sides. But I must remind you also that we expect the same of China. They have no role here,' said Johnson.

'Have you told them?' asked Chong.

'No. We expect that you have your own framework with reference points peculiar to your own population make-up. You are on your own in that respect. You have to make clear to China, if you do not have a working relationship with them already on this matter, that this is a purely South-East Asian enterprise and, to repeat, that China has no standing in this matter.'

'Mr Ambassador, we will do what needs to be done.'

'I am sure you will. Thank you, Mr Prime Minister,' said Johnson.

'Good evening, Mr Johnson.'

'Good evening.'

Steven Chong remarked to Dr Wong in the Blue Room that the American ambassador had carefully avoided calling him Steven as he was wont to.

★

Dom Thomas had decided to move into Tessy's flat in Tiong Bahru for the duration, and as they reached home after the St Andrews experience the telephone rang. Tessy's contacts had tracked down Peng Ah Pat's latest address, and it was a pleasure for Dom to talk to his old friend again, even if only on the telephone. He was not a rolling stone anymore, he said.

'I have middle-aged children now,' Peng explained.

But his wife was twenty years younger than him and they had been together almost ten years. The best thing to come out of the conversation was that Peng had an old 45-rpm record player for his opera collection. And he also had the only known copy of *The Portuguese Fisherman's Daughter*, which used to be a favourite of the group in their heyday, and it used to be in all the jukeboxes in the bars. They would get together one day and play it again as they used to.

'And, hey, Dominic. I want to see pictures of your family. Okay?'

'Sure,' Dom said, and remembered that Peng had always referred to him as Dominic, never Dom, like his other friends. '*You're not a liqueur*,' he used to say.

★

All evening the television had been displaying code words in the continuing call-up of national servicemen: *Salt Palace, Farm Gate, Rough Sea, Old Shoe, Animal Farm, Iron Shed, Cool Hand, High Note,*

Hard Hat, Chain Saw, Cycle Chain, Mirror Image, Music Scene, Big Bus, Blue Shoes…

'Some of those codes being bunched together means they are going into action,' Tessy said.

And the television continued, this time repeating words broadcast a few hours earlier: *Uncle George, Red Roses, East Garden, Iron Gate, Cold Iron, Large Castle, Shoe String, Zinc Cover, Sand Castle, Clear Sky, Jungle Noise, Thin Wire, Smooth Voyage, Narrow Road…*

Rose said that the NCIP was saying that China had already warned Malaysia not to launch reprisals against its Chinese population.

'What's the NCIP?' Dom asked.

'National Chinese Internet Programme, initiated by the Singapore government. Sometimes you get news here that you can't get anywhere else. Only, it's all in Mandarin.'

★

Back in the Blue Room, the consensus was that Singapore should initiate talks with Malaysia first thing in the morning. To pave the way, there was work to be done during the night. The UN Security Council had to be persuaded to call for peace talks, the Australians had to be brought in as go-betweens. It was considered essential that talks be started before the Malaysians launched a major offensive. Then, it would be loss of face to stop the fighting.

'They have sweated it out for two days,' Steven Chong told the gathering. 'They may be amenable to talks now. I have already spoken to Canberra. We will have to wait for the morning for further developments.' Then he turned to Dr Wong. 'It may be time for one of your famous historical trivia, Dr Wong. We need a little relief from this stress.'

'Okay. Did you know Cleopatra was Greek?'

'I thought she was Egyptian. Tell us the story,' said Chong.

'It goes like this. Alexander's troops rebelled over his unending quest for expansion after his last great battle, in what is today's Pakistan. By then the Macedonian had led a Greek army to victory over the hated Turks and Persians and many points south and west. He turned back and travelled west, but he died in Babylon, what is today's Iraq, probably from a poisoned arrow which had sneaked past his armour and pierced him in the armpit during the Indian battle. His generals seized their chance and transformed themselves into rulers in many of his conquered lands, one of which was Egypt. Ptolemy was one of these Greek generals, and he is reputed to have reburied Alexander in, yes, you guessed it, Alexandria; and he established himself as the first Pharaoh of a new dynasty on the Nile. Sadly, one of the undesirable royal customs of the Egyptians that the Ptolemys adopted was that of brothers marrying sisters, and Cleopatra was the end result of 300 years of this kind of royal incest. She was a very beautiful woman, living in a palace full of cripples and mental defectives, and she played a role as a power-broker in Rome, before she came to an untimely suicide to end the Ptolemy dynasty. And she did not kill herself because of a broken heart, but that is another story.'

'Thank you, Dr Wong. I needed that. Call General Fong to brief us on deployments south of Kota Tinggi and Kulai.'

Chapter Six

On the other side of the Causeway that Sunday, Jaffar Ibrahim went to the *istana*, the palace, and was met by an elderly adviser to the Sultan. They moved to the veranda where a table and chairs had been arranged. The garden was in splendid shape. The orchids were all in bloom. A retainer brought in tea and biscuits and withdrew.

The Dato was a patient man, he waited for Jaffar to say his piece. Yes, he was aware that the palace was now within Singapore territory; yes, he was aware that this placed the Sultan's position in some ambiguity.

'Therefore, Dato, the following proposal might find some favour,' Jaffar continued. 'Singapore is offering the office of the President of Singapore to the Sultan. His Highness will be Sultan of Johore and President of Singapore. The two can be linked so that whoever becomes Sultan also becomes President. I think the proposal offers great honour and prestige to our Sultan. It also sets in concrete the future of Johore royalty. I would like you to present this proposal to the Sultan. My Singapore contacts are expecting a response today itself.'

His Singapore masters, Dato Mustapha told himself, then said to his visitor, 'Before I approach His Highness I would like to say a few things. I do not think there will be a positive response because I am aware that the Sultan is furious at the loss of a large piece of his state to a foreign invasion force. In that state of mind anyone should think twice before approaching His Highness with a proposal to join with the enemy. He may go for his firearm. He has already handed out weapons to most of the people in the palace, and he is in a military mood. I, personally, do not think Singapore will be able to hold this territory for long. The battle has not even begun, from Malaysia's side. I think Singapore should be thinking about how it can extricate itself out of this mess, because the war could come to their city.'

'But will you at least present the proposal to the Sultan? I can wait, if necessary.'

'Let me see if I can find him.'

Jaffar sipped the tea and wondered how the Sultan's gardeners managed to keep the lawn so thick and emerald-green. Stella would be waiting for his call, and other luminaries in Singapore too would be waiting anxiously. If the Sultan agreed, it would be a coup they could crow about, and one that would bring great rewards for him, Jaffar and Stella. They would make a very successful couple. Dato Jaffar had a nice ring to it. *One must be flexible in coping with the uncertainties of life. Who would have thought that Singapore would one day presume to launch an attack on Malaysia and seize part of Johore? The old Causeway that had linked the two countries is now just another roadway.*

The Dato returned to the veranda in his slow ungainly walk. His face was blank.

'I am instructed to inform you that the Sultan has no response. You got it? No response.'

'Does he want more time?'

'No. His response is: no response. And I don't think you should come here with this proposal again.'

'Dato, you are not in Malaysia any longer. You are part of Singapore. You have to listen to them.'

'Eventually, after the dust has settled, we will have to see about the future. You should read Hang Tuah and Hang Jebat again.'

'Yes, Dato. So there is nothing more to talk about.'

'I am afraid so.'

'*Selamat pagi*, Dato.'

'*Selamat pagi*, Encik Jaffar.'

Within the hour he was in Stella's arms. She wanted him to keep pressing the Dato and the Sultan for a few more days. It was too early to throw in the towel. In any case, she could see that they, that is, Jaffar and herself, had many new opportunities in Johore.

*

The two officers from the *USS Harry S. Truman* who arrived by helicopter, landing on the padang in front of City Hall, were driven straight to the US Embassy for a meeting with Steven Chong, who had brought along Dr Wong and a Mindef officer, Colonel Siva Manickam, the latter to provide a multiracial front, for Chong was aware that the ambassador had remarked on Singapore's excessive Chineseness.

The ambassador, a youngish man with a full head of grey hair, had eight embassy officers with him, and Cohen was among them. They were in the study, and Lieutenant Tom Ettridge and Lieutenant Bill Thompson were escorted to their seats without much ceremony.

Ambassador Johnson invited them to address the gathering. Ettridge seemed to be the senior and he began: 'Look, what you have here is a minor spat that you can sort out yourself. What we are concerned about is that third parties should not get into the act.'

As a matter of fact, the Americans were a third party, Chong told himself.

'There have been certain movements of ships, planes and missiles in China which we believe is to do with this military operation. China will be dissuaded from interfering, and that may bring about some tension. But we must all steer clear of unnecessary rhetoric.'

'We don't need anybody's help. What makes you think China has a role in our part of the world? They have never ventured outside their borders,' said Chong.

'I suppose India and Vietnam were aberrations. But if there is great distress in Singapore, don't you think there is the racial affinity to help? We are here to inform you that you should not expect any help from China, even if they wish to and you issue an invitation. Whether you succeed or fail will depend on your own resources,' said Ettridge.

'That was always the way it was going to be. But excuse me, do you have any reason to anticipate great distress in Singapore?' asked Chong.

'War is an unpredictable thing, sir. All I am saying is that we have noted some unusual military movements in China, and we can only link them with what has happened here,' answered

71

Ettridge.

'By the same token, can you make sure that Indonesia keeps out of it?'

Johnson: 'There is nothing to indicate that they want to get involved.'

'Are you saying that one aircraft carrier can stop a country like China?' enquired Chong.

'Not stop entirely, just the power to do sufficient damage so as to make the caper not worthwhile. You must be aware that we also have access to instant back-up,' said Ettridge.

As the meeting broke up Cohen escorted the two officers to the private quarters for drinks and lunch.

Chong reminded Johnson of his promise to attend the President's charity concert, and as soon as they got into the car Chong asked Colonel Manickam about the *Truman*. From an inside pocket the officer pulled out a sheaf of printouts, and Chong was impressed.

Commissioned 1998. Cost US$7.3 billion, carrying eighty aircraft including S-3a Vikings (anti-submarine hunters), F-14 Tomcats (fighter-bombers), E-2c Hawkeyes (radar planes), F-18 Hornets (strike fighters), and HH-60Hs and SH-60Fs (anti-sub helicopters), and presumably carrying nuclear weapons. In theory, she could go on circumnavigating the globe without stopping until 2018, thanks to two nuclear reactors. It produces its own fresh water by a mix of recycling and desalination. The Truman will spend its entire life span at sea, for there are only two or three ports in the world that can accommodate it – twenty storeys high from the waterline and 150,000 tonnes. Its motto is the same as President Truman's when he was in office: The Buck Stops Here.

Chong wished he could get an invite to visit the ship and dine with the captain. That would be an experience.

Dr Wong finally brought up the subject that was uppermost on their minds. The China angle was 'for us to know and for them to find out later, much later,' but they already had. That had been the ace in Chong's pack, the possibility of China throwing its weight behind Singapore's legitimate and historically justified efforts to safeguard its water supply. The months of talks in Beijing had produced a result that Singapore considered positive, for China had agreed to make threatening moves to intimidate the Malaysians in recognition of the huge sums of foreign exchange that Singapore had brought to China's development. In addition, Chong had taken the precaution to brief the Americans in advance of Operation Temasek. What game were the Americans playing? What had they told Suleiman Bakri?

'Let's move the action to the United Nations quickly,' Dr Wong said.

Chong agreed: 'Yes, the more we talk, the better. We must give the new border time to settle. Suleiman must have seen the steel and concrete we are putting into it.'

★

There was tension in Kuala Lumpur that Sunday. There had been more racial incidents in the capital, Seremban, Ipoh, Penang, Kota Bharu and Kuantan, but they were considered minor outbreaks; no one had died in the incidents. The people were becoming restless, and Suleiman understood their frustration; Malaysians were not prepared to give up an inch of their land.

'Our war begins tomorrow,' he told his Operations Room. 'We are taking the fight to the Singaporeans inside their city, not in the Johore jungle. They are going to get a nasty shock. What we have to do is to withstand calls to halt the fighting as soon as things get hot for Singapore. China's power in the Security Council can operate against us, unless, of course, we can pre-empt that by accusing them of intending to misuse their veto power for the benefit of an aggressor nation. So, contrary to what the Singaporeans might think, considering all the noise we have been making out there, we are not placing too much faith in the United Nations. We will fight to win, and then we will think of the United Nations. What Singapore did was naked aggression, and what sort of reaction did we get from the so-called civilised countries? A lot of meaningless words and no action. Even the Indonesians have had very little to add to the debate apart from some saintly words about not rewarding aggression, softened by talk of Singapore's need for water. They still hate us. Sukarno's Confrontation never ended for them.'

Curfew was imposed on Kuala Lumpur at midday Sunday after a tense stand-off between two groups in Chow Kit Road.

This time tomorrow most Malaysians will have something to celebrate, Suleiman told himself.

★

Word had spread that Dom was back in town, and he got a call from Samuel Liew, retired petition writer and now a life insurance salesman. Sam was married with two daughters, both in the civil service. Dom and his friends had always treated Sam with extra consideration because Sam was one of those unfortunate people blessed of a handsome face but without anything resembling a neck, for his head with its long face rested on his shoulders. He was known in their company as The Lost-Neck Monster. But he turned out to be healthier than most of his contemporaries, for he still played golf. Sam had another claim to fame: neither he nor any member of his family had ever bought a Japanese product – car or stereo or computer or anything with a Japanese name, and they never would.

'I know a Jew who will never even sit in a German car,' he used to say. 'Why should I give the Japanese the benefit of my custom?'

Dom asked Sam if his attitude had changed after all these years.

'No,' he said. 'Have you read Iris Chang's account of the rape of Nanjing? Wholesale massacre, for days on end. I believe it is called a *datushai*. I've never told you this before, because it is very painful for me. I have an Indian friend and he told me what his grandfather saw during the occupation. He worked for the Domei news agency, the Japanese outfit, trying to undermine the British war effort in Burma. One day his Japanese boss invited him to witness something he said he would never see anywhere again. They were in Penang at the time because that was where they were broadcasting from. The two men went to a street corner in the middle of the night, and suddenly both ends of the street were blocked by trucks and armed soldiers. Everyone in the houses were ordered out in the state they were in, some naked, some in briefs. Men, women and children. When all were on the pavement, they were ordered to walk to one end of the street where there was a row of five or six hooded men, each with a long stick. As the people went past the hooded men would point with the stick and the people were separated, some into lorries, some on foot to the beach and some back to their homes by another route. The ones who were marched to the beach were all beheaded in an orgy of samurai-type sword play. Men, women and children.

'The same thing had happened earlier in Singapore. Here it is called the *Sook Ching* massacre. It means *Wipe Out*. I lost an uncle and his family that night in Penang. Two cousin brothers and a cousin sister. But I learned about it only years later. The whole family clammed up because, apart from anything else, it was also a shameful thing because there was no way we could avenge their cruel deaths. My friend's grandfather witnessed the terrible spectacle on the beach and there was nothing he could do about it. He learned later that the people who were taken away in the lorries were tortured by the Kempeitai, the Japanese version of the Gestapo, for details of freedom fighters. Some years after the war my friend's grandfather came to suffer bouts of amnesia, and he couldn't work. This is an eyewitness account of a *datushai*. So why should I buy a frigging Japanese transistor?'

Dom wondered who the hooded men were.

*

At two sharp, Asma Latiff was out the door, walking briskly down the three flights of stairs. She turned left near the air well and walked the short distance where a survivor of the old ways had a vegetable garden. Near the back fence, in a corner behind a clump of papaya trees, was an old tin shed, covered with dirty old plastic sheets. She could tell from the disturbed earth that someone had already lifted the plastic. She guessed right. Mohammed Ariff had got there before her, parking his small Toyota a little distance from the farm, and he was already checking the cargo inside the old Bedford van. Neat wooden crates, plastic boxes, round wire casings. Neither spoke, but Mohammed Ariff remarked that there wasn't a speck of dust on the stuff.

He took the key from the glove box and turned the ignition. It fired instantly. He let it run for a few minutes, checked out the gauges, and then shut the engine. Asma in the meantime was rearranging the crates, three on each side, wires at the back, and all linked to a little box. She put new batteries into the box, wrapped it in an old rag, and placed it gingerly between two crates. She threw a large carpet over the whole thing, and then they drove back to Asma's flat and she brought down a pile of her clothes, all on hangers.

They returned to the farm. This was the tricky part. They had to move the clothes through the farm and into the van without anyone noticing. The farmer had been paid not to pay any attention to the goings-on, but there were others. Luckily, the farmer's wife and two children had gone to the shops, so the operation turned out to be relatively safe. They quickly hung the clothes on pre-fixed lines inside the van, and set about the final task. The CK Tang logo had already been outlined on both sides of the van. They filled in the colours, and that was it. The hair on Asma's neck prickled with excitement as she walked back to her flat, while Mohammed Ariff, sucking on a joint, drove to see someone in Arab Street before he went home, *probably to buy some more of those things that he smoked*, Asma thought.

Although the job of preparation was done, Asma was aware that her accomplice was a disturbed young man, mainly because of the sexual tension between them. Whenever she had run into him, on the stairs or on the void deck where there was a weekly library, she was aware of his eyes on her. He had come a little too close to her and brushed her thigh when they were in the van. She had chosen to ignore the thing and carried on her work without saying a word. Then, as they were loading the clothes inside the van he had suggestively put his hand on the bodice of one of her garments. She had laughed it off. Then finally, in an act that could not be mistaken, he had put his hand on her shoulder, and, for the first time, Asma had had to speak. She had told him, in Malay: 'My husband is a policeman.' Under different circumstances she might have allowed him some liberties, for he was very good-looking and a good ten or fifteen years younger than her. *Well, we all have to make sacrifices sometimes*, she told herself.

★

Ah Ching was at that moment also making his way back to his flat. There was an audible wheeze as he walked, but his job was done. He was operating alone. He had walked to a godown in one of the old buildings beside Singapore River where he too had worked on an old Bedford van which carried the same cargo as Asma's van. But Ah Ching's van was filled with suitcases, all with airline tags. Each bag had holes drilled underneath, and all were linked by wires to a little box wrapped in cotton and lying hidden inside the stack of suitcases. He too had put new batteries in the box. His final task was to fill in the colours of the name and logo of Raffles Hotel, etched in outline on either side of the van.

Ah Ching walked at a quickening pace despite the tightening in his lungs, for his girlfriend was spending the night with him, as she occasionally did. Since they could not go to the movies and eat out, Mui Fong had told her parents that she might as well spend the night in Ah Ching's flat. In any case, it was in a safe area. And they were going to get married. Eventually.

A smile flickered a moment on Ah Ching's face when he thought of the polytechnic girl who had made violent love to him on their second date. She called him Queensland, for its bananas, and he called her *Chilli-padi*, for an extremely hot variety of chillies.

When Asma got home, she discovered four things in quick succession. Her two children were not there; they were spending the night with Mohammed Ariff's mother in the next block because the old woman's grandchildren were all with her for the duration; Mohammed Ariff was sitting in her husband's favourite armchair near the window; and her husband had left a message on the answering machine to say that he would not be coming home for at least another twenty-four hours.

Asma could feel Mohammed Ariff's eyes on her, and she had that tingling feeling at the back of her neck.

'*Kismet*,' he told her.

'My foot,' she said, without conviction.

He opened the small package lying on the table and spread out the most magnificent necklace she had ever seen. She couldn't tell whether it was real gold or real stones, but… She looked into his eyes and she could see the yearning, or was it that stuff he had been smoking?

'Please Asma,' he said, falling to his knees.

And Asma was suddenly young again, the eighteen-year-old on her wedding night, back in steaming Kota Bahru.

'God forgive me,' she said, moving towards the bedroom.

Chapter Seven

There was high tension and deepening worry, for everyone realised, as night and curfew descended on Singapore, that the morrow would be decisive in many ways. The city was an eerie sight: brightly lit but empty streets, and the audible hum of millions of television sets and computers. Although Singapore had the means to control and vet the Internet, a sudden upsurge of websites and the massive volume made things difficult for the government's moral-political enforcers. The thought police had suggested that the only alternative was to shut down Internet access altogether, a step vetoed by Steven Chong. So now the information explosion was in full sway. Insult heaped on hate, and obscenities proliferated in many languages, sometimes romanised and with English translations; racial jokes from the bottom of the filth barrel.

Steven Chong's son telephoned to say that he had noticed that Malaysia and Singapore had been replaced by Malay and Chinese in the angry exchanges. Nationality had been subsumed under racial *tsunami*s. Very quickly a barrage of non-Chinese names appeared on the scene, all attacking the lazy Malaysians. They did not miss a beat in KL, and a similar wave of non-Malay names appeared, talking about Chinese deceit. The old masters of *wayang kulit*, or shadow play, were at it again. And it was obvious that the whole exercise of name-calling had descended into farce. The jokes played themselves out eventually, but the chat rooms were still going full blast; some websites had been flamed out.

It was well past midnight when the arguments began to manifest some seriousness, without the obscenities and racial vilification. AzlanMalik said that if it was true that many years ago Prime Minister Tunku Abdul Rahman had threatened to shut off Singapore's water supply to teach it a lesson when Singapore was part of Malaysia, then in hindsight it appeared that he should have done the deed, not just threaten to do it. That would have been a fork in the road, said someone calling himself or herself April-May, for no one could say if the Chinese in Malaysia would have stood by and watched Singapore wither and die on the vine. There would have been an uprising that the British, Australians and New Zealanders would have been unable to cope with, while China would have been forced to become a major player in the piece. That was not to say that China had not now become a major player, but many matters left unresolved at the time of Singapore's eviction from Malaysia would have been settled. A partition of peninsular Malaysia even, to accommodate its Chinese population, preferably in the south adjacent to Singapore, like the India/Pakistan partition. That would have laid the groundwork for a great Singapore nation, something that was now being attempted with water as the slogan.

Unfortunately, AzlanMalik said, *in your dreams, you...* Not one inch of Malaysia was for the taking by anyone; when the crunch came, Singapore would be the new Beirut. The word sent a shiver through Singaporeans who read what AzlanMalik called his 'assessment' of the situation.

AprilMay replied that many inches of Malaysia had already been taken. If they had been vigilant, it would not have been so easy for Singapore to have achieved their objectives within a day and without much bloodshed. So they might as well stay on their side of the border and behave themselves. Singapore was entitled to secure its water supply, and it was not reasonable for Malaysia to expect that threats to cut off the water supply would not eventually force Singapore to take action. The country was financially strong enough to cope with Malaysia's unfriendly actions on the currency and share market fronts, even the occasional closing of its air space to the Singapore Air Force; but water was a different matter. *Hang Tuah will getcha*, AzlanMalik said. *Bruce Lee will bury him*, said AprilMay. *They are both dead*, said SmallChicken. *Godzilla will chew up Empress Place*, said MatSalleh. *Ukay Heights will sink into the sea*, said HotShot. And so on and so forth.

AzlanMalik asked what the Malaysians were to make of the Everest business.

'Two Malaysian Chinese men working in Singapore climb the

mountain and what flag do you think they planted on the peak? The Singapore flag.'

AprilMay asked, 'Why not? They have jobs and a future in Singapore. They were being kicked around before they came here, and the expedition was financed by Singapore sources.'

Maps of the so-called Mersing Line, with pictures of troops behind defensive barriers were now beginning to appear on the Internet. The troops appeared to be lounging nonchalantly with not a sign of any opposition. There were video clips of the CIQ (Customs, Immigration, Quarantine) booths being dismantled at the old Causeway and Tuas crossing points. Makeshift facilities were already going up on the tollway and the other, older, highway going north.

Word of these spread quickly and millions of terminals were downloading them. Cheers rang out in some HDB towers as the significance of the pictures began to sink in. More than all the talk, the pictures showed in graphic form what Operation Temasek was all about. You could see that the pumping stations and the catchment areas were all now within Singapore's control. There was plenty of land left over for the new factories and housing estates that a blossoming Singapore would require. The images they created in one's mind were too dazzling to describe.

All through the night this feeling of euphoria, that of a great victory in Singapore's history having been achieved, began to permeate the island. With China in the back pocket, could anyone stand in the way of Singapore's glorious march into the new millennium? Yes, Harry Lee had got us started, but he had always been at a disadvantage because of the trauma he had suffered when the Tunku told him Singapore was being ejected from Malaysia. What might have been, had always plagued him. Steven Chong Yoke Lin carried no such baggage on his back. He could see what Singapore needed, and he had the courage to go out and see that Singapore got it.

But for all that cyber-activity, it was a typical Singapore night. And sex was high on the agenda for this curfew-bound population. An older autocratic regime used to deny its very existence, and extramarital affairs led to dire political and career consequences for high profile personalities. Possession of even mildly pornographic material, videos and magazines, still remained punishable by the courts, although there had been some relaxation of the dress code for nightclub acts and stage shows. 'So long as the private parts were covered,' skin was tolerable.

Singapore men had always found release in Bangkok's Patpong and further afield in Chiengmai and Phuket, followed closely in their popularity by the fleshpots of Manila and Jakarta. But the economic rigours of recent times had led to a more localised search for sexual fulfilment, now being pandered to by a discreet network of premises. Sex was beginning to rear its head again in the more respectable venues, with increasing numbers of casual relationships blossoming in bars and clubs. This was the evolving Singapore. Liberalising gradually without going overboard. But tonight, though, there was a certain desperation in the air as the population paired off for the night.

*

Larry Lim downloaded more of Lingling's pictures and lapsed into his own little erotic world, consummated when his own ball of fat finished putting the children to bed. Aileen knew about his fixation with Lingling, but she considered it a harmless pastime, so long as she herself stayed fat and happy and capable of keeping his interest. Easy that was, for she was naturally plumpish and born with a good humour. She told Larry she got her name from a song her mother heard on the radio the night before she was born, *Goodnight Irene*.

Her giggles could be heard from the street, but she didn't care. Neither did Larry. On the other side of town, Peng Ah Pat was lying on the carpet listening to old records of Chinese opera. The words rose and fell in typical spurts of the Chinese *wayang*, or street opera, accompanied by the peculiar *doom-doom-cha* of drums and cymbals. He, too, would have a happy consummation in due course. But he knew that for him the thrill of the chase was over. His last conquest would be his last. The parade of past victories in his mind brought an involuntary smile. No, he wouldn't have done it any other way, he told himself. Then, for old time's sake, he put on a record he hadn't heard in a long time. *The Portuguese*

Fisherman's Daughter. Too bad Dom couldn't be there.

Dom felt that way, too. For his old friend called him, holding the phone to the antique hi-fi so he could hear the old melody again. We will do it again soon, they told each other.

Tessy brought out the scotch and they lounged on large cushions on the carpet for another long night of R&B and jazz, watching out for Important Statements on the television.

'Whatever happened to Bugis Street?' Dom asked, mixing his own drink.

'They're a class act now,' Tessy replied. 'The place has been done up as a tourist attraction and there's no violence. And you wouldn't believe they are not women. I don't know if it is the better make-up or the lighting or the clothes, but the boys are really beautiful these days. Rose and I took some overseas friends there for drinks a few months ago, and the women were dumbfounded at the curves on display.'

'Hey, Rose. Don't feel so bad. They're no competition for real women,' Dom suggested.

Rose, at the computer, laughed.

'Stupid arses,' she said.

'Arses, yes. Stupid, I don't know. They say they're following their natural inclinations,' said Tessy.

'Men are from Mars, women are from Venus, and these things are from Uranus,' said Rose.

'Actually, Dom, nothing much happens in the old haunts. I believe a nearby field is the pick-up point now,' said Tessy.

'As I said, they're all from—' Rose was cut short.

Just then an Important Statement interrupted an old Roy Rogers western on the television and Tessy turned up the volume.

Why, it was a pretty Malay lass this time, and she urged the population to try and not take their cars to work. There would be plenty of buses to cope with the shutdown of the MRT. The burden was further eased because educational institutions would remain closed for another day.

★

Janet was spending the night in Nick Cohen's apartment. He was going to be late but not later than midnight, he had said. So she donned a new outfit in red satin and curled up in front of the television. As things stood, the curfew would be lifted at 6 a.m. and all offices and services were to be resumed, except for educational institutions and the MRT, or the light rail network. Buses and taxis would be back on the roads. The banks and the Stock Exchange, and all related financial services, would open as usual. The people were urged not to rush the supermarkets and overstock on groceries. There was plenty to go round, and the people should avoid panic buying. The fresh produce markets would have stocks only by about lunchtime.

Janet listened to the succession of Important Statements and wondered if there wasn't an element of *Alice In Wonderland* about all the hopeful talk. Were the Malaysians really going to sit back and allow a chunk of their country to be taken by Singapore? She had been able to get through to an aunt in Petaling Jaya and she had said that Chinese people she knew were in a state of terror because the Malays were talking about the Chinese having grabbed a big piece of their country. There had been some disturbances but nothing major, but she feared the worst. Malay soldiers were said to be worked up about having let the territorial grab happen.

Janet thanked all the gods she could think of for her safe haven in Singapore. Safe? Haven? For how long? Her brother was spouting the government line that there would not be any further military action, that peace was the focus of government initiatives. Watch things happen at the United Nations, he had said. She had her misgivings, and Cohen had agreed with her assessment. The worst was yet to come.

It was about 10 p.m. when Cohen got his opportunity to do something, anything, in the unfolding scenario. The ambassador wanted a low-level transfer of a piece of information to the Singaporeans, and Cohen was low enough in the hierarchy, yet diplomatically on the inner track; and Cohen chose the Deputy Defence Minister, Saw Chee Keng, to establish links because they had met at a function only a couple of weeks earlier and Saw had appeared to be a well-read, articulate person. Cohen was put through to the Deputy Minister quickly.

'Yes, Mr Cohen. This is an unexpected pleasure. What can I do for you?'

'Nothing actually, Mr Saw, but my government would like to know whether you are aware of certain aircraft movements in Butterworth.'

'I am not privy to such military information, Mr Cohen, but tell me what you know. I will pass it on,' replied Saw.

'Two Harrier fighter-bombers have turned up at the Butterworth base from the north. They are carrying full armaments, and a short while ago they took off to the west and are flying south over Sumatra. There are no markings on the aircraft, and we do not think they are British, and you must know that Australia and New Zealand have never had Harriers. You may be forced to cross into Indonesian air space if you think they are a threat. A ticklish situation, I would say. Anyway, my government thought you should know,' offered Cohen.

'Thank you, Mr Cohen. I will pass it on. No doubt, your diplomats in KL would also have this information. Have they had any new contacts with the Malaysian government?' asked Saw.

'Not since yesterday when they accused us of complicity in Singapore's actions. Our denials have not been taken seriously. And since then, you must be aware that China has warned Malaysia against taking reprisals against its Chinese population. A provocative action on China's part, we think.'

'We cannot tell China how to act. On the other hand, China may have legitimate concerns for the safety of Chinese people in Malaysia. A warning would put the Malaysians on notice that China is not a passive party, that the welfare of people of Chinese origin wherever they may be is a matter of interest for the Chinese government.'

'We were hoping for the reverse, that Singapore's actions would be looked upon as being nationalistic. China's entry would give it a different slant,' said Cohen.

There was a pause, then Cohen continued.

'May I rephrase that? China's entry at this juncture would give the Singapore action a racial overtone.'

'We are hoping to avoid the racial element, too. We are presenting a multiracial front in this matter,' Saw stated.

'Yes, we have noticed. But is it not just that, a front? Your word,' enquired Cohen.

Saw laughed.

'*Touché*! Give it another twenty-four hours, and we will get a clearer picture of Malaysia's intentions.'

'To be sure. Good night, Mr Saw.'

'Thank you, and good night, Mr Cohen.'

Within minutes, Saw was calling his liaison officer at Mindef, while Cohen got on the phone to the embassy in Kuala Lumpur, for diplomats from America, Britain, Australia and New Zealand, in addition to the Japanese and diplomats from other Asian countries were also trying to find out how the Malaysians were going to react. The relative inaction was surprising, although it was known that Suleiman Bakri's political standing was a little shaky. Cohen learned nothing new, and he decided to call it a night. He phoned Janet to tell her he was on his way.

*

Very quickly, Steven Chong, too, was being briefed about the Harriers. He was still in the Blue Room, and they were all confident that their surveillance of Malaysian aircraft was foolproof. The American tip-off had been an eye-opener. Harriers are VTOL aircraft, for vertical take-off and landing. The pilots must have used that technique to sneak their aircraft into Butterworth. But whose were they? Not many countries had Harriers. That question would have to wait. The immediate concern was that Mindef required a political decision to take military action beyond the present theatre of conflict. It was no longer a question of the Indonesians staying out of the fight: they must be persuaded to close their air space to the Malaysians. Otherwise all bets were off. The tight geography of the region predicated that action would spill across borders.

'Where are the planes now?' Chong asked.

'Near Palembang, and they appear to have veered further west in an extended holding pattern,' said Colonel Fung.

'Testing us?'

'Could be. Should we talk to Jakarta?'

'Or shoot first and ask questions later? Can we be accurate enough to bring them down outside Indonesian air space?' asked Chong.

'If they wish to attack us, they need not leave Indonesian air space. Today's stand-off weapons can be fired from great distances,' Fung informed him.

'Are we certain that they are Malaysian aircraft, or at least doing the job for Malaysia?'

'We can be fairly certain of either supposition, sir. We need a decision whether we should challenge the two Harriers over Indonesian air space to either drive them away or force them to act. Either way we would have a rationale to bring them down. But Indonesian reaction is critical, for there is always the danger that their planes will take to the air to defend their territory. That would be justified, of course, but that would complicate the situation for us in many areas.'

'Yes, yes, Colonel, I am aware of the implications. Still, I am of the view that we should have a quick hit on those two Harriers and get out of the area before Indonesian fighters can react. Then we can try to explain that there was no time to seek Indonesian permission. We will inform the Indonesian embassy here of the incident after the hit. The Deputy Minister will summon the ambassador and explain to him that it was not the intention of the Singapore government to intrude into Indonesian air space but that it happened inadvertently in the heat of the action. Hot pursuit, and all that. What do you think?' enquired Chong.

'Yes, it might work.' *Or it might not*, the colonel told himself, but he was not going to tell that to the Prime Minister.

Chong required Blue Room endorsement, which was forth-coming within the hour.

But in that time the two Harriers had gone east and were approaching the island of Borneo, where they could wheel north-west and head for home, avoiding Singapore and American recon aircraft. So the order to the RSAF was that the two Harriers would be downed if surveillance aircraft thought they were in attack mode, a subjective undertaking.

Nothing further to do but wait, Chong told himself. He had no fears about the RSAF's ability to bring down the Harriers, because Singapore had the deadliest and technologically most advanced fighters and bombers in the region.

Unknown to a population drifting off to sleep after a long night, matters were moving in unforeseen directions, for a partisan Indonesia could be a real handful.

★

Changi Airport stayed open throughout, and the harbour continued working non-stop to keep the shipping lanes moving.

'That should help us maintain a semblance of normalcy,' Chong remarked. 'Which reminds me, Dr Wong, would you have another piece of historical trivia to break this unremitting tension?'

Yes, Dr Wong had. He had prepared one in his mind, for he had been convinced that another trivia request would not be long in forthcoming.

'I shall tell you something about East Malaysia. You know, the Malays claim to be the largest single racial component in Malaysia, but that is because they have counted all sorts of other people as bumiputras, which, of course, is true, in a manner of speaking. But they are not Malays. Like Melanaus, Bahaus, Dayaks, Ibans, Penans, Kadazans, Bidayuhs, Kelabits, Kenyahs, Kayans and scores of other ethnically different people in East Malaysia. Which is why one of our working papers suggested that Sabah and Sarawak might be amenable to an approach to form a federation with Singapore.'

'Good one, Dr Wong. Do you think we can have one more?'

'Let me see. How about this? I will tell you how the dollar sign of two uprights with an "S" going round them came about. It actually comes from the Spanish dollar, from the "pieces of eight" of pirate stories. On one side it showed the Spanish shield with the so-called Pillars of Hercules on either side. One of these pillars was the minaret of the Moorish mosque of Seville, which became the bell tower of the Cathedral of Seville after the Moors were driven out. Similarly, the other pillar was the minaret of the Arab mosque of Damascus which too became a cathedral when the Spanish held Damascus for eighty years. These two pillars had ribbons in an "S" form around them, saying Seville and Damascus respectively. They were called the Pillars of Hercules because it was believed that anyone who controlled them also controlled the area between them, in this case the Mediterranean, a critical piece of water in those times, and which endowed on Spain an aura which may be equated to that of a superpower in today's terms.'

'We should have prominent markers at either ends of the Mersing Line. Yes, yes. All in due course. Not that we have superpower ambitions!' said Chong.

There was laughter and applause in the House.

Chapter Eight

'This is ridiculous,' said Connie, a diminutive blonde with great big hazel eyes, as she cleared the glasses from the tables on the back patio. She was in such a state that the magnificent orchids in bloom failed to catch her attention.

The little patch of grass was a gleaming emerald backdrop as the sun glinted on diamonds of water. Her husband, Peter Chapman, the English bank manager, had been watering the garden while talking to his guests, since the gardener hadn't put in an appearance for two days. Helping Connie was Leslie, the wife of David Russell, the Australian stock analyst, and Patricia, the wife of Ossie Eisenberg, the American hedge-fund executive.

What was ridiculous for Connie was that the main attraction in Peter accepting the Singapore job offer had been the fact that she would not have to do housework. Between the three families they employed no less than six maids, three gardeners (part-time) and two drivers, and all had deserted their employers, moving into little ethnic fortresses only they knew.

The maids were Indonesians and Filipinos; the drivers were Singapore Malays, and the gardeners were probably illegal immigrants from Bangladesh. The expatriate women were all in agreement that as soon as things quietened down they were going to make things uncomfortable for the agencies that provided the foreign maids. And if the women bothered to return, they would be told to go back to their homelands on the first flight out. They were needed now, but they were all probably shacked up somewhere, having a good time.

'I'm not going to wait to find out if my two maids are pregnant,' Connie said. 'I have no intention of taking the responsibility. I'm sure you would have been warned about it. A maid getting pregnant is supposed to be the responsibility of the employer. There's a lot of money involved, like penalties and loss of a deposit.'

'Yes, I know,' said Leslie, a strapping redhead, with faint echoes of her natural Strine, or Aussie accent. 'We are thinking the same thing. We might as well get new maids.'

'Pity, really,' said Patricia, with not a trace of her Bronx origins. 'I had just about taught my girls how to run a proper American household. Esther, particularly, is very good. I only have to help with part of the cooking, she will do everything else. Cutting the vegies and getting everything ready for the cooking, then laying the table and serving and everything.'

'My girls are also quite efficient,' said Leslie. 'They make sure the children are fed on time, no matter what time we get home. That's always late because I have to go with David to these little corporate things they are having all the time, and they want stock analyst types like David at these things.'

'Well, we better get used to making do without these luxuries,' said Connie. 'We hadn't a clue this sort of thing was in the offing, and the London head office is saying a man in Peter's position should have known something as big as an invasion of another country was about to happen. But what about the diplomats? I hear several governments had been briefed before the invasion. They could have given us a whisper. Nothing. They think they belong to a higher class, not like us mercantiles.'

'I know what you mean. I had lunch with a commercial attaché's wife the day before the invasion, and she didn't say a word. They must have known,' said Patricia.

'Not necessarily,' Peter shouted from the garden where the men were trying to identify the orchids. 'Men don't tell their wives everything.'

'Why not? You think we're all blabbermouths?' asked Patricia.

'That commercial attaché's wife would have been making a mistake if she had told you. That is, if she had known about it in the first place. It's sensitive information that has a huge market value. The entire Holland Village network of expatriate wives would have been in the know within hours,' said Ossie.

'Your hedge fund can expect some losses.'

'Yes, a little. Surprise, surprise. We were out of this market and a few others a week ago. The decision was taken on factors that had nothing to do with this military thing.'

'I agree with you. I had made similar recommendations a full ten days before the invasion, but some of my clients were tardy in taking action. Some did, though, and they'll be thanking me,' said David.

'I'm afraid that if they do open the market on time, there will be a massacre. Unless, of course, they use government funds to buy in. Who's selling and who's buying in the first ten minutes will tell you a lot about the state of the market,' Peter offered.

'Foreigners are all likely to be net sellers, and local institutions the buyers. But the market will still take a dive and I'm afraid a lot of local investors will get spooked and lose a motza,' predicted David.

'Don't you think the nationalist spirit will boost the market?' asked Ossie.

'Look, when it comes to money, they're all individualists. The nation can look after itself, let me look after myself first. That's a universal thing.'

'Yes, mate. They're all the same everywhere when it comes to money,' agreed David.

'Heard from the kids yet?'

'Yes. They're okay. All five are with David's parents in Sydney. They were tired out after the flight, but kids have this remarkable ability to bounce back quickly. They are going to the beach somewhere up north today.'

The kids were Connie's two and Leslie's three, all aged between eight and twelve, students of the American School, packed off to Australia for the duration.

The phone rang and Connie picked it up.

'Yes, I'll get him,' she told the caller; then, 'It's her again.'

She mouthed the words to Peter.

He didn't like the way she said it, a suggestion of unnecessary and frequent contact with someone she did not approve of. But he bit his tongue and let it pass. Connie had been getting worked up over Elizabeth Lam for some weeks now. London and Hong Kong were getting impatient about the lack of any direction from their man on the spot; Elizabeth was his shock absorber, and she needed to speak to him often in these trying times. Whatever other relationship he might have with Elizabeth, they never allowed it to intrude into business or family affairs. They were soul mates only on their fortnightly trips to Bangkok or Hong Kong, on bank business. The arrangement suited them fine, and the Chapman household functioned as any expatriate home should.

'She has a big butt,' Connie whispered to the other two women.

Leslie and David Russell were aware of the other woman in Peter Chapman's life, and they had sworn to themselves never to do or say anything to break up the family. Hopefully, Peter would forget Elizabeth Lam when he returned to England. They themselves were in a constant state of rowing and making up, for both suspected the other of having affairs. Not true in his case, but unfortunately true on Leslie's. She had met this exercise guru at the gym, and the next thing she was going to his flat in Katong every Tuesday and Thursday afternoons. He had an Italian name, but everyone was convinced it wasn't his real name. They were right; it was Kernail Singh, former physical education teacher. Friends had once taken him to Zouk, the nightclub, and a place called Venom the following week, and he had seen the possibilities, for several women had eyed him. But nothing much had come of it. So Kernail had discarded his turban, hacked off his long hair and his beard, and gone to the barber for his first haircut and shave. He had burst in on the world as a hunk called Tony Cadenza, six feet tall, with broad shoulders, snake hips and a smooth line on the importance of exercise.

Monica's Health Centres had hired him immediately as the house guru, and very quickly he had advanced to part-owner, for Monica Tham was an admirer. Among others.

Tonight, for the first time in four years, he was home; home being his widowed mother's terrace house in MacPherson. His older brother and his family, and his younger sister, were all there. A strange night to bring together a splintered family such as theirs. Splintered by bickering after the older brother married a Chinese university lecturer and the sister expressed the wish to marry a Canadian airline pilot.

Some time during the night Kernail Singh, too, would be called up. He had no speciality the armed forces could use, and he had not done well in training, so he expected to be in the artillery carrying the heavy stuff on his shoulders. He was surprised they hadn't called him up earlier.

Back at the Chapman residence, Peter opened another bottle of wine and Connie put on the Madonna CD.

Pat and Ossie Eisenberg had problems of a different sort. She couldn't have children, a fate particularly painful for a Jewish woman. Adoption had failed to appeal to them on very basic religious grounds, and they had not been keen on the new medical procedures that could have produced an acceptable outcome. Surrogacy presented the least risk and was within her own religious boundaries, she was told, but she had declined that too. Now they were well past thinking of such things; they just muddled on, rudderless, accepting postings all over the world and partying into the night. The dinner he hosted at the aquarium was still the talk of the town.

All these different strands of life came together under one roof that night, reaching a crossroads of some sort.

Another Important Statement on the television and more code words for the national service call-up.

'What do they need more men for?' David Russell asked, and provided the answer himself: 'Probably for sentry duty. They must be afraid of infiltration by commandos. And there is so much shoreline to cover.'

*

Tessy and Dom were into the last quarter of the bottle of scotch when Rose pulled out an old record.

'His girlfriend used to sing this in the old Bukit Bintang cabaret,' she told Dom, indicating Tessy by a nod of the head. 'He thinks I don't know. She was older than him, and still he used to run after her. Dom, you remember her?' Dom did, actually, but he chose to feign surprise. 'You his friend, lah. You can bluff,' Rose said with a laugh, and she put on the record, *Unchained Melody*.

Tessy listened stony-faced. *I hunger for your touch…* Dom wept, for he had his own demons to battle. *Time goes by so slowly…* And when it was over, the silence was finally broken by Rose: 'I'm sorry, lah. I forgot about your own pain. I wish I had met her.'

Another Important Statement on the television. Yes, it was confirmation that the curfew would definitely be lifted at 6 a.m.

★

The *Truman* had been tracking the two Harriers long before they arrived at Butterworth. They had taken off again and if they stuck to their present course they would pass the carrier only a few kilometres to the west. An unwelcome intrusion. Then the unexpected happened. The Harriers called the *Truman* and requested permission to land. The skipper obtained approval from the Seventh Fleet Commander and the *Truman* pulled aside a few of its helicopters to make room on deck.

The Harrier pilots were unmistakably British. They said *hello* to the first officers who came up to the aircraft, and they just stood near their aircraft beaming, as more Americans gathered to take a look at the new arrivals and their aircraft. For it is always a strange sight to see a Harrier coming in to land. It will jet in like any fighter, slow down to a standstill and hover before settling down like a helicopter. The two pilots did some stretching exercises.

'Beautiful ship you got there,' one told an officer who appeared to be the seniormost.

'Yeah, but please identify yourselves.'

'Flying Officer Carruthers, and this is Flying Officer Stannard. We are part of the British presence in the Middle East. We were told to give the Malaysians a helping hand.'

'Just the two of you? And why no markings.'

'These are actually Malaysian aircraft. We sold them this morning.'

'Anyone could have brought you down, you know. The Singaporeans were getting a little disturbed by your presence. What can the two of you do?'

'Confuse and confound. They have a real headache in Singapore now, I believe. We'll be off now. Mission accomplished. Say thanks to the skipper.'

The American officer spoke into a communications device clipped to his collar, then told the visitors: 'We could have been forewarned through diplomatic channels.'

'Yes, I agree. But this is how matters panned out. Malaysian request.'

★

Another briefing for Steven Chong.

'Whose are they? Why did they land on the *Truman* if they were not American? Why no markings? And where are they now?'

Colonel Fung counted four questions in the one breath.

'They gave us a wide berth and flew back to Butterworth where they are inside a hangar,' he told the Prime Minister.

'What is going on? Are the others in the Five-Power Agreement taking sides? You realise, if the Malaysians have any more of these Harriers, the bombed-out runways are not going to stop them,' said Chong.

'Yes, sir,' said Fung.

'Have we spoken to their military attachés?' asked Chong.

'Yes, sir. But they are saying they know nothing, or have nothing to say,' Fung informed him.

'Order greater vigilance, especially in the air.'

'Yes, sir. Orders have already been given.'

Chong called for Dr Wong, who was napping in a chair in one of the rest rooms.

'Needs careful scrutiny and analysis,' Dr Wong said, when he learned of the Harriers' progress. 'We must not be hasty and take any action that might infuriate our allies. By allies I mean the Americans, the British, Australians and New Zealanders. They are the only ones who will have a role to play in finding a lasting peace. But no peace without water for us.'

'Yes, of course,' agreed Chong.

'Did you call Suleiman Bakri again?' asked Wong.

'Yes. He repeated what he said earlier. That we must pull back into our island and start negotiations on a new water agreement. I told him that would be futile. Malaysia has demonstrated repeatedly that it had little respect for agreements, particularly water agreements with Singapore. The only way to settle the matter is for Singapore to keep the land it has occupied and pay Malaysia a sum of money based on an equitable land value. We can afford to pay, and they desperately need the money.'

'That is true, and what was his response?' enquired Wong.

'He uttered an expletive.'

★

Malaysia's generals were becoming restless. The enemy had been squatting on their territory for forty-eight hours, and confused signals were coming from the Ops Room. But regardless of Suleiman Bakri and his wishy-washy colleagues, the Malay Regiment had already taken action. For two nights troops had been marching through jungles and plantations, in a single arrow, coming down the high ground of Malaysia's central spine, without armour and without air cover. But they had a plan. A fist right on the button in the middle of the Mersing Line, and then quickly push south in a narrow line. That would spread panic among the occupiers to know that the Malay Regiment was already behind them. From the air they would never be able to tell who was who in the trees.

The Malay Regiment was made up of career soldiers, always kept in fighting trim, while the Singapore forces were mainly national servicemen with a twenty per cent leavening of full-timers. Singapore's artillery could open up in a deadly barrage, but they would never know if they had their own men in their sights. A static force would always be at a disadvantage in the tropics because of tree cover, something the jungle-bashers of the Malay Regiment intended to use to the maximum to spread confusion while moving south as fast as their legs could carry them. There would be casualties, and the troops on both sides were unaccustomed to that inevitable consequence of war. Malaysian forces had had a peaceful history since Indonesia's Confrontation ended and the communist insurgency died off, but they were still a committed force, fighting for their own country, unlike the occupiers, a polyglot force more used to the good life.

★

Ismail Sebi informed his Prime Minister some time during the night that the Armed Forces planned to hit the Singaporeans at first light on Monday morning. Like in the song, it would be one fist of iron on the Mersing Line and the other of steel inside Singapore. Further, there would be confusion in the air, with one Harrier flying west beyond Sumatra and south, going to the extent of its fuel and landing at an Indonesian base.

'We have Indonesian permission for that,' Ismail Sebi said, anticipating the Prime Minister's query.

The other Harrier would fly east well past the *Truman* and head south, eventually landing in Labuan. These distances would draw away a fair number of Singapore aircraft, and they would have to go all the way back to Singapore to refuel. Mid-air refuelling would be risky at these distances.

'A tricky situation for them, and they would never be able to make up their minds whether to attack the Harriers or not. They know that Malaysia has never had Harriers, so they'll be reluctant to open hostilities with some other country,' Ismail Sebi said. 'All we need to do is sow the seeds of doubt in their minds. The Malay Regiment will do the rest.'

'The Malay Regiment? I thought they were to wait until after our little fireworks in Singapore?'

'Yes, sir. But I am afraid that in this instance they have to follow their natural instincts. They have to act, sir, regardless of anything else that you might be doing. After all, the Singaporeans are on Malaysian soil. One of our senior generals grew up in Kota Tinggi,' said Sebi.

Suleiman Bakri was sure that the generals had out-manoeuvred him, but somehow he felt relieved. He was unhappy that it was his Internal Security liaison officer who had brought him this information. The generals should have told him. Did they think he was vacillating? He could be as tough as anyone, but he was not foolhardy. Now the generals were taking action on their own, so he would not have to take the responsibility if things went wrong. But the glory, of course, would be his, if they could inflict a decisive blow on the Singaporeans. Yes, Suleiman Bakri liked the turn of events. He now had the opportunity to try and heal the deep schism that had afflicted Malay politics since the upheaval at the end of the twentieth century. They needed to redefine themselves as a people and a nation for the uncertainties of the new millennium, he told himself; the Singapore invasion might turn out to be a wake-up call for them.

Suleiman Bakri's thoughts turned to coining some choice phrases for his victory speech. He called his old friend Samsuddin Salleh for help. The man was almost eighty, but he still had a sharp mind and he was well respected for the speeches he used to write for two former Prime Ministers.

Despite the hour, Samsuddin Salleh set to work. The old warhorse had his own axe to grind, for he had had a minor role in Umno's disputes with the PAP during the time when Singapore was a part of Malaysia. He had hated the PAP's 'intellectual' arguments against his 'racial mathematics'. He had been having his own revenge for some years, though, until the exertion had become too much.

It happened like this: he had come to know a farmer who lived in a village in the upper reaches of a certain river that fed the catchment area of Singapore's water supply. He would visit the farmer every few months for a mutually satisfying ritual; the two men would go for a walk, past the tapioca and sweet potato patches, the rambutan and papaya trees, the clump of banana, the durian plantation, and finally the sugarcane on the waterside. Then the two men would ceremoniously urinate into the little stream. Samsuddin Salleh does not forgive or forget.

Chapter Nine

The last time Dom had seen the man was in a *yum-cha* place in Melbourne, and he had been singing Mandarin songs on the karaoke. It had been an unusual experience, listening to this *gwei-lo* or *ang-moh* singing duets with one of the Chinese waitresses. And he had done it quite well, too, for he had received loud applause. And here he now was, in the Chinatown Complex in Singapore eating in one of the claypot-rice stalls, the one run by the Lim Sisters. The guy obviously had local knowledge, for the Lim Sisters' claypot was supposed to be one of the tastiest in the business. Dom went up to him.

'I'm Dom, and I'm *also* from Melbourne.'

Dave did not miss the emphasis on *also*.

'Good on you. I'm Dave.'

'We dropped by for some takeaway. This is my friend Texeira. You need any help?'

'That's very kind of you,' Dave said. 'But I'm all right. Let's exchange telephone numbers, just in case. I'm Dave Mitchell.'

'Okay. I'm Dom Thomas.'

When they reached Tessy's home, Dom wondered aloud that it was too much of a coincidence to run into a Mandarin-speaking *gwei-lo* in the middle of a little war in Singapore/Malaysia.

'The game's on,' Tessy said, matter-of-factly.

'What game?'

'The game played by the secret service. Spies, 007 types. There must be many angles to this little war.'

'You realise that no one has actually declared war? I would have thought that at least the aggrieved Malaysians would have declared that a state of war existed with Singapore.'

'Yes. It's all funny peculiar,' remarked Tessy.

★

David Mitchell had pulled off the deal of his life. The nature of his work in the grey areas of military intelligence with contacts right across the entire spectrum of the business had provided him an opening to do something he'd never done before. He had approached the Malaysians with an offer they couldn't refuse, under the circumstances. Then he had gone to the British with an offer which they, too, found too good to refuse. He just wanted a four per cent commission, from both parties. The deal was for twelve Harriers with full armaments and add-on missiles. The Malaysians could use them despite the loss of their runways, and the British could make a lucrative sale with the prospect of continuing ordnance sales. What was more, the British had everything the Malaysians needed in the Persian Gulf, and could make immediate deliveries.

The Harriers were to arrive in flights of two at a time so as not to attract too much attention, to be accompanied at intervals by three C-130 Hercules with more bombs and missiles, and spares. Deliveries would be complete by Monday night, and Dave Mitchell would be a very rich man. His commission should be in his account in Zurich by about lunchtime Tuesday, seven or eight p.m. Singapore time. Then he would be gone. He knew the Americans were furious; he thought they had failed to make some quick sales, and they didn't like being outsmarted. They would be trying to figure out a way to make something out of all this. Desert Storm had turned out to be pretty lucrative, in more ways than one. And there's always more ways than one to skin a cat. The *Truman* must be costing them a packet.

Dave Mitchell was right. Late that night helicopters brought the heads of eight missions to the *Truman* from Singapore and Kuala Lumpur. Two each High Commissioners of Britain, Australia and New Zealand and the two American Ambassadors. There had to be an understanding that no attempts would be made to inflame the situation further. Britain was of the opinion that any settlement that left Malaysia a loser would only set the stage for a more devastating confrontation. Then there was the question of the Harriers.

'Yes, but they only helped to create a more even playing field,' Sir Leighton, the British High Commissioner in Kuala Lumpur, asserted. 'In any case, the deed had been done at a higher level.'

'You know,' Johnson said, 'we could have sold Singapore a whole lot more stuff, but we didn't.'

He felt aggrieved. The British had always had more acute commercial instincts, although it was inarguably true that American hardware was far superior and technologically more advanced. Also, the British appeared to have more friends, otherwise they could never have pulled off the Harrier deal.

Johnson studied the diplomats' faces closely; *nothing to be gauged there*. No one mentioned American missiles being flown to Malaysia: did they know, or were they keeping the information to themselves? The Australians, at least, must have guessed what those long crates with US markings were that were being quickly moved away from Butterworth's runways. And the British, too, for their pilots had arrived with the Harriers. Anyway, Johnson hoped that there would be no more arms sales. With that unanimous agreement, the meeting broke up. Drinks with the skipper, then back to their posts.

While the diplomats were winging back to their stations, a new phenomenon was unfolding on the Mersing Line, late at night. Thousands of little lights appeared, coming up to the bunkered troops from behind them in clusters; torchlights, bright pump-up kerosene lights, and low chatter. Hot Hokkien noodles, satay fresh off the glowing coal, cold soy drinks, fruit juice. And girls. Anywhere along the line you could have a warm meal, maybe even a bright-eyed lass to break the boredom. 'Twenty dollah.' Singapore dollars, of course. Every war in every century had seen them, the camp followers.

The generals and officers cruising the lines were furious.

'This is a farce. Get them all to go back at least a kilometre,' Brigadier General Soh Huck Cheng screamed at his adjutant, who shouted at the platoon nearest him. 'And pass it on.'

The general went among the frontline entrepreneurs, and an odd mix of cooking smells and cheap perfume tickled his nose and made his eyes water. He wondered if he could suss out a spy or two among the hawkers and the enterprising young women, each with a pillow, blanket and mosquito net and rolls of string to tie up the net, the whole thing in a neat bundle on the back like a rucksack.

'This won't do,' he kept muttering to himself. 'This was never the way it was going to be.'

If real fighting broke out his men could get caught with their pants down, literally, and the hawkers and hangers-on would only get in the way. Headquarters wasn't impressed, for what he was seeing extended coast to coast. The goings-on on the beaches were simply outrageous. Everywhere, the smells of hot food and the low hum of humanity making the best of the situation.

Apart from all the niggling things that were beginning to clutter up the general's neat military mind was the sudden appearance of twenty-four foreign tourists demanding to be sent on to KL, for some had pre-booked railway tickets to Bangkok. That would not be; he sent them all to Singapore and they would have to make other travel arrangements. Then there were the entrepreneurs from Singapore trying to get into Johore, trying to buy real estate. Sentries at the old crossing points had already been instructed not to let them in. A Singapore identity card would be enough to be told to go back. And that was in spite of the intimidating sight of large numbers of troops and heavy guns and missile batteries that had been moved in to defend the Tuas bridge and the Causeway, together with its water pipes and the railway line.

The general was worried about civilian casualties in Johore in the event of a full Malaysian attack. There had been some movement of people over the Causeway into Singapore, but there was a limit to how many people Singapore could accommodate. Most of the newcomers were moving in with relatives or friends. That was as far as Singapore was willing to tolerate. Tent cities for refugees were out of the question. The question of sanitation had been considered and found too expensive. On the Mersing Line itself, Soh had insisted on portaloos all along the line and the troops had been supplied with toilet tissues.

'We won't make a mess of our environment. We are Singaporeans,' the General had told his men.

There would be defining moments on the morrow, the General knew. His men would be getting the real taste of war for the first time. They had been trained adequately, they were physically fit and strong; they had superior weaponry, and every effort had been made to fortify them mentally.

Had they overlooked something, the General wondered. The population appeared to have accepted the fact of Singapore capture fairly quietly, but then the population was almost seventy per cent Chinese in these parts, and local Chinese had always had an emotional attachment to their successful brethren across the Causeway. But they were not into joyous celebrations yet, for it was still unclear if the Mersing Line was permanent. If the Malay-dominated Malaysian forces came back, they would not be forgiving if the locals had been too friendly with the invaders. So they waited, ready to move to escape the fighting when it came.

★

Two more Harriers landed at Butterworth, and an hour later the first Hercules arrived. Then at half-hour intervals, the rest of the aircraft arrived. And all went under cover in the hangars immediately. The British pilots were to return to their station in the Gulf in one of the big Hercules aircraft. Malaysia was fortunate that six years earlier twenty pilots had been trained for the Harriers, but the deal had fallen through and the RMAF had opted for the American FA-18s. A few flying hours, and the Malaysian pilots would be ready to take the Harriers into action. But they were aware that the Singapore pilots had been trained and upgraded constantly in the United States, Australia and even France, and should not be underestimated. Malaysia's 'fly boys', as Singapore pilots called them, would also be put to the final test. One must expect that apart from the new Harriers, the rest of the RMAF would be in play if the runways were allowed to be repaired. The RSAF decision, then, was that at the first sign of any offensive action in the air, a full attack would be launched to destroy Malaysian aircraft on the ground. The success of that would have a direct bearing on any action on the ground or at sea.

Singapore had the resources for the job; by the late 90s the RSAF already had fifty F-5s, between sixty and ninety A-4s, and undisclosed numbers of F-16C/Ds and F-5EF Tiger IIs. Then there were the swarms of attack helicopters. A small island nation like Singapore never really needed this level of firepower; not for defence anyway. The Malaysians should have known that.

★

Some time during the night, Cohen received a call from his ambassador, and he called Deputy Defence Minister Saw immediately. Despite the hour he got through instantly.

'My apologies for calling you at this hour, Mr Saw, but my government would like to pass on some information that may be of interest to you. Maybe you already know this, but more Harriers have arrived in Butterworth and the runways at Subang and Kuantan should be repaired by morning.'

'Thank you, Mr Cohen. I will naturally inform my government of your kindness in letting us know about this new development. Is there something we can do for you to show our gratitude?'

'Well, nothing actually at this time. But depending on how things go, you might keep in mind that the *Truman* might at some stage be useful in a peacekeeping role,' said Cohen.

'Thank you. We will keep that in mind. Insurance, you might say,' said Saw.

'But we will be strictly neutral. You must not expect us to do anything that might compromise our neutral position. But third parties would be discouraged, otherwise this action might be the spark for a bigger conflagration.'

'What do you mean?' asked Saw.

'The effect on China. Not all of China is pulling in the same direction, as I understand it. Independent action by some faction is a likelihood if Singapore descends to any distress. You see, Mr Saw, we are not entirely certain about the control and command structure of the Chinese armed forces at this time. And I am talking about pretty powerful stuff.'

'I am sure we won't reach that situation, Mr Cohen. We can take care of ourselves.'

'And remember, the *Truman* will always be there, if you need us.'

'Need you? Are you making an offer of assistance?' asked Saw.

'Not exactly, but if things get out of hand and the United Nations calls for a ceasefire, and this applies to both Malaysia and Singapore, the *Truman* might be available to play the role of the cop on the beat to keep the peace,' said Saw.

'Ah yes, the cop on the beat. The United States has considered itself the policeman of the world for some time now. I say that not as a criticism. You have done a great job. But as I understand it, you needed to be paid off the last time.'

'What do you mean?' Cohen asked.

'I believe the Saudis and the Emirates had to pay through their nose for your help in keeping Saddam away. And they are still paying, I believe.'

'I hope you are not suggesting extortion, but the fact is that our defence expenditure is huge, Mr Saw, and we try to ease the burden on the American taxpayer wherever we can. With that in mind, beneficiaries of our defence capabilities will be offered avenues for some recompense. No compulsion, of course. We know, for example, that the British have been able to make very lucrative deals on military aircraft and armaments with the Malaysians in the last forty-eight hours.'

'We are aware of that. But you must know that almost all our aircraft, helicopters, missiles and anti-aircraft defences are of American origin. It is just that we don't think we need any more at this time. We are well-prepared and well-stocked,' stated Saw.

'Yes, it is good to be well-prepared. There is one other thing. My ambassador wishes to inform you that he expects the Malaysian High Commissioner and his staff to be treated in a manner strictly in accordance with the code of diplomatic protocol. We are passing a similar message to the Malaysians regarding Singapore's diplomats in KL.'

'Thank you for that. On our part, my Prime Minister has instructed us that we will always maintain a civilised attitude in our dealings.'

'Yes, I am sure, but believe me, Mr Saw, some of the worst and most mindless atrocities of war have been committed by people and governments that espoused the highest thoughts of civilisation. I hope you won't take that to mean that I am questioning your sincerity, because I'm not. Anyway, I am heartened by your assurance. I shall pass that on to my ambassador.'

'And I to my Prime Minister, the gist of our conversation.'

'Good night, Mr Saw. Oh no, good morning.'

'Yes, of course, good morning, Mr Cohen.'

Cohen had omitted to tell Saw that some American missiles had been delivered to Butterworth, and quickly moved out under tree cover near Seremban. If Saw knew about it, he too had not mentioned this development. Singapore had no anti-missile defences, and Malaysia was not known to have long-range ground-to-ground missiles, other than normal combat missiles and anti-aircraft batteries. Well, Singapore could be in for a few surprises.

★

Steven Chong was intrigued. What did the Americans want? *We will win the day no matter how high the Malaysians push the stakes. That is, providing the Malaysian action is confined to the mainland.* There would be no bomb craters in Singapore, and the republic had the surveillance facilities and aircraft to ensure that. He knew about the Harriers and the Hercules and Galaxy aircraft arriving at Butterworth. Armaments for the Harriers. *Well, when we get going there won't be much left.* The Australians had been informed that while Butterworth was off-limits to Singapore Air Force aircraft, any Australian aircraft that took off from Butterworth would be considered a participant in the action and dealt with accordingly. So, while Singapore kept a close eye on movements at Butterworth, the main targets were the Subang and Kuantan bases.

'Is anyone here from the air force?' Chong asked, and an officer wearing the red lion emblem of the RSAF approached the Prime Minister. 'Are there any new developments?'

Brigadier Liew Sook Yoon said, 'None, sir. The air crews are being briefed right now. We will be ready for all eventualities.'

'You know that Malaysian soldiers are marching south well away from the roads? The High Command thinks Kota Tinggi in the centre will see heavy action,' said Chong.

'I believe so,' said the Brigadier.

'Well, we have done all we can. Get some sleep, gentlemen. I want you all here at 8 a.m. By that time the curfew would have been lifted for two hours, and whatever action the Malaysians intend to take would be on. By about 10 a.m. I think we will know how things are going.'

★

Dave Mitchell called Dom just when 5 a.m. alarms were going off all over Singapore, to be ready to get out of the house when the curfew was lifted at six. Dave wanted a favour: could Dom find him a place to stay for a couple of days? Dave didn't say why or how he came to be in this predicament. There were plenty of hotel rooms available, well then why? Tessy offered to take him in himself, if it was only for a couple of days. So that was settled. Dave would come over when taxis got back on the roads. His problem was that he needed to wait until he could get confirmation from Zurich about his money, but he had to lie low while he waited, because all through the night he had been getting this uneasy feeling. If the cheesed-off Yanks let on to the Singaporeans that he, Dave Mitchell, was the one who engineered the Harriers deal for the Malaysians, some pretty unpleasant things could happen to him. Hotels were unsafe for a man in his position.

'I'll make it up to you, mate,' Dave told Dom.

'I'm sure you will, but I'm not insisting,' Dom told him. 'Texeira is my friend, and he'll do anything for me. And listen, don't ever call him Tessy.'

'Okay. I like him. He's so different from the chuppies I've been dealing with.'

'What? Chuppies?' asked Dom.

'Yeah, Chinese yuppies. There's big money in these parts, and these cocky young men wear Italian shoes, French shirts, English suits and talk about *Les Misérables*, just to show that they know how to pronounce it,' replied Dave.

'What do you do for a crust?'

'I'm a salesman. You needn't know more. I'll be out of your hair ASAP after I get word that the transaction has been completed. Not more than a day or two.'

'Okay. But why not move into a hotel?'

'I don't like the competition.'

'What about us? Is there any risk for Texeira?'

'Oh, none. These are purely commercial matters.'

'Okay. See you in a couple of hours. But remember, you shouldn't put any of us in danger,' said Dom.

'Believe me, there is no danger. Everything I do is strictly legit,' said Dave.

'If you say so.'

But Dom was beginning to get an uneasy feeling that maybe the guy was bad news. And yet, it would be unfair to assume the worst and throw him out in the street. In any case, one is never happy about business practices in these parts, especially at times like these. Businessmen have paid with their lives when deals turned sour, but he knew of none in Singapore itself. So long as you stayed clear of politics and drugs, Singapore was a fairly safe city, quite unlike Bangkok or Jakarta, Manila or Hong Kong. But Singapore had its peculiarities, enforced with a passion only authoritarianism of a peculiar bent can muster; no littering, even cigarette butts; no jaywalking, no shaggy long hair, no spitting, no smoking in most places, and no chewing gum. Fines were instantaneous. Graffiti could get you at least three of the best, a *rotan* or cane on your backside. A copy of *Playboy* in your luggage could put you in deep trouble. That was Singapore, and unlikely to change.

★

Over in Geylang, Asma Latiff wept when Mohammed Ariff went back to his flat, three storeys down, at about two in the morning. Her orderly and ordered life was entering uncharted territory. She herself had been changed forever by the events of the night, and her life would never be the same again. That is, if she was still alive the next day. She thought of Ah Ching, the intense young man who never spoke much, driven by sheer hate. How would he cope, now that the real action was upon them? Would he do something stupid, like driving too fast or cutting lights? The operation could be jeopardised if he had an accident. It had been drummed into him about the danger the smallest traffic violation could pose. She didn't like the dazed look that descended on him sometimes. Was he on something? Mohammed Ariff didn't think so. Still, it was a worry.

Ah Ching, meanwhile, was lying in bed looking up at the ceiling as his *chilli-padi* breathed softly beside him. He wondered whether he should wake her up one more time. He went to the kitchen to get a drink and when he came back Mui Fong was sitting up.

'Thirsty work, eh?' she teased.

'Yes,' he replied, 'and I am going to get even more thirsty.'

Chapter Ten

All Singapore forces had been on full alert for imminent attack since midnight Sunday. The men on the Mersing Line and the beaches were keeping their heads down and peering out into the night, which was at its darkest in the hour before dawn. Their electronic listening and tracking devices told them there was movement out there, fanning out in an arc from the central hills, but there appeared to be millions of targets for the radar to lock on to.

'They must be spreading transponders which attract radar and other electronic target-acquisition devices,' Captain Wee Tong Soon remarked to his sergeant.

Captain Wee and his platoon were on Mersing's eastern fringe, with the beach to the right. In front was the river, its black, whispering water gone quiet, the unmoving balance of the tide at its peak just before it turned. He heard the low murmur of the Hawkeye early warning aircraft flying high over the ocean, moving north in its lonely quest. He and his sergeant held the centre in the line of twelve men facing the water. Sergeant Low Eng Guan squatted beside his machine-gun, set up on a rock pile, as his captain studied his map once more with a pencil torch. The rest of his men were spread out to the right and left, each with a tree or hole in the ground for cover and protection. There were also prefab concrete barriers which unfortunately offered a ready target for attack, so the Captain made his own defence line well away from them.

Similar initiatives were being taken by other platoons all along the river bank to the beach to his right, and right across the small town and into the plantations and jungle to the other coast. There had been a grenade attack during the night at Kota Tinggi, well south of their lines; a jeep had been destroyed with two dead and three injured. Headquarters had concluded that it was a local job; the Mersing Line was tight. Still, the level of vigilance along the lines was stepped up.

The captain was thinking about his bride of six months in her father's flat in Bishan when he saw a faint flash in the sky far to the north-east, followed a few seconds later by a low, rumbling blast.

'I think the Hawkeye's got it,' he told his sergeant. 'Soft target, probably all they can manage.'

It was the first explosion he had heard on this operation, apart from small arms fire from Singapore troops shooting at any perceived movement on the other side. As far as he knew, there had been no return fire. Most of the action had been far away, at the Subang and Kuantan air bases, now gone silent for the next step: escalation or negotiation – war-war or jaw-jaw, as Mao would say.

Private Hwang Eng Tian lit a cigarette, although smoking was not encouraged in the Singapore Armed Forces. He was sitting on the ground, with his back to the tree and his SAR21 between his legs. He heard his captain saying something to his sergeant. It was still too dark, starlight merely covered the treetops with a light touch of gossamer. Just like the time they had spent in East Malaysia, trekking in the Mount Kinabalu area. That was something. With the cigarette hanging from his lips, he took out a bar of chocolate from the outside pocket of his shirt and began to roll back the foil, slowly and neatly. That was as far as he got. The thin knife went into his heart in one neat thrust. He never saw anything, he never heard anything, and he never made a sound. The silent slaughter began on the riverside and spread east to the beaches; by now there was shouting and firing, but it was impossible to tell the enemy from your own men. If one had the time you could tell from the smell; Malaysian marines had crossed the river, swimming and wading through the stinking ooze on the banks.

Sergeant Low ran his torch up and down the riverside; nothing. He switched on the powerful searchlight against his better judgement and scoured the water; nothing, just coconuts bobbing in the water. He tried the other shore; nothing. He turned the light back on to the water, and now he noticed something. Did that coconut jerk suddenly? Was it his imagination? The Captain had seen the movement too. They let loose with the machine-gun, and they killed eight marines who sank into the water with the coconut husks still around their heads. All across the lines there was firing, shouting and cursing. They couldn't tell how many Malaysian marines had come ashore, but the net had closed and a search was on. Sergeant Low had that adrenaline-high gleam in his eye as he searched the water again with his search-light. There was that stink again, and the sergeant looked around.

'Hey, captain, can you smell something?'

Sergeant Low peered hard at where he thought his captain was; nothing. Where could he have gone? The sergeant felt the wire round his neck a split second before he joined his captain on the other side.

More shouting and shooting, further back behind the lines.

'We've cornered them,' Corporal Kuo Min Hwang whispered to the soldier who carried the cameras and the tiny transmission box.

'You shooting anything?'

'No, sir. I could get my head blown off if I turned on the camera lights.'

'Okay. Start shooting as soon as it's daylight.'

In an hour or so they would be able to see the first streaks of purple and the day would dawn pretty rapidly. In the meantime, they would stay quiet and keep their heads down. But that was not good enough for headquarters. The Blue Room was of the opinion that the intrusion should be ended quickly, but that was easier said than done. The mud and swamp were too much. The platoon commanders considered calling in the amphibian personnel carriers, but they could get bogged down. Dangerous if the enemy had mortar; they would be sitting ducks. Finally, they called the air force for assistance, reluctantly, for there had always been friction with the more glamorous branch of the force. The helicopters failed to pick up anything and returned to their job of guarding the Causeway and the second crossing at Tuas.

As the Chinooks were reporting negative, the word from the ground was disturbing. Thirty-two Singaporeans dead, three injured; four Malaysian marines confirmed dead and another eight shot and believed dead, none captured.

'That was a bad one for us,' Steven Chong remarked to Dr Wong in the Blue Room. 'But our lines are still intact. We will have to hunt down the remaining marines.'

'Yes, Mr Chong, but I must warn you that there is likely to be more bad news before the day is out. I don't think this little raid is all the Malaysians can throw at us.'

'Headquarters thinks so too. Their runways would have been repaired and they should be able to mount an air offensive if they wish. You know, of course, such an offensive would be snuffed in their air space, and their entire air force would be destroyed, in the air and on the ground,' said Chong.

'Yes, I know, but we have achieved our main target: that was to bring within our control the catchment areas of our main source of water. Everything that happens from here on will be to defend that position and work towards a peace settlement that sets it in concrete. I would say that we must start that process right away,' said Wong.

'Thank you, Dr Wong. I am truly grateful that you managed to convey that thought to us without mentioning the words *paradigm shift*, and such other words as *ethos* and *dialectics*.'

There was suppressed laughter from Nancy Lim and Brigadier Tan who were close by, for the philosophy doctor was known for lapsing into cloudy language sometimes. Then Chong said, 'Not funny ah? Anyway, in a few hours the Americans and the Australians will be speaking to Suleiman about the need to find a quick solution without further bloodshed. I, too, will try to speak to him. I would suggest face-to-face talks in any neutral venue. The *Truman* comes to mind.'

'What is the word from the United Nations?' asked Wong.

'The Chinese representative has been active on our behalf, trying to persuade Security Council members to call for an immediate ceasefire. The strange thing is, the major powers do not seem to think the time has come for that. Do they want a few thousands to die before they think the time for a ceasefire had come?'

'Could it be a reaction to China itself?' suggested Wong.

'You mean, the more China pushes, the more the resistance towards our own position?' exclaimed Chong.

'Exactly. On the other hand, we must make full use of China's veto power. That works for us, not for the Malaysians.'

'By about midday we will get a clearer picture. The Malaysians must be mad to risk destruction of their air force. If they take offensive action, it has to be understood that as far as their air force is concerned, it is all or nothing. I cannot risk an air strike on the city.'

'I'm sure they know that. So what happens next will be the act of a desperate man, or a more calculated ploy. We must always be conscious of the Indonesians. They can turn against us at any moment. I have said this before, and I know our air surveillance of the south has been without incident. What do you read into the Malaysians knocking out the Hawkeye?' asked Wong.

'I welcome Brigadier Liew Sook Yoon to repeat, for the benefit of the members of the Blue Room, the briefing he gave me a short while ago.'

'Thank you, sir. We believe it was a missile that brought down the Hawkeye. It was a quick strike, from Kuantan. We have, of course, sent a flight of eight F-16 Falcons to knock out any missile launchers they can spot. We have done a fair bit of damage around the air base, but it is doubtful if the Falcons hit any missile launchers. All their planes are still parked in full view. We can take them out any time. The Falcons are being prepared for the next mission and I am to inform you that the air force is at full operating capacity, loss of the Hawkeye notwithstanding,' said the Brigadier.

'Thank you.' Then to an aide, a young woman recently graduated from Harvard, Chong said, 'You will take care of getting Suleiman on the line for me at about 11 a.m. He should be awake by then.'

There was laughter, for it was known that Suleiman Bakri was a late riser.

'Certainly, sir,' Nancy Lim told him.

★

The two bridges across the thin sliver of water separating Singapore from Malaysia had always had greater significance than they merited, mainly because the border between the two countries also bisected the two structures, until Singapore changed the borders by force of arms. The Causeway is actually a land bridge, whereas the other bridge is an example of modern engineering, soaring across the water in a bold sweep with broad entry and exit roads.

Both were heavily guarded: six Chinooks, flying east-west in two groups, three companies of national servicemen led by a full colonel, supported by two anti-aircraft missile batteries and banks of cannon and machine-guns, backed by the nearby Singapore naval base.

Precisely at 6 a.m., just after dawn, the first missile came from the north, hitting the railway line at the Singapore end of the Causeway. The next one hit the Causeway itself in the middle, cutting the road, twisting the railway line and bursting the giant water pipes. The machine-gunners opened up towards the expanse of water to the east, not knowing what they were shooting at, but they had to do something. Water cascaded from the pipes from two sides. The third missile was aimed at the other bridge, but it overshot, destroying fourteen shops and killing and wounding a large number of people. The fourth missile missed the bridge by a few hundred metres and fell into the water to the west. Then the fifth missile hit the Causeway again, almost at the same spot as the second, creating a larger hole but not much more damage. The sixth missile hit the Tuas bridge at the base of the span rising from the Singapore end. The bridge withstood the blast, but there was now a noticeable list to the left; it could topple over at any time.

Singapore had no instant reply to a missile attack of this sort, for its limited anti-missile defences were in a few critical sites within the city. The helicopters and the Colonel and his men watched helplessly as their mission blew up right before their eyes. Four dead, eight injured, all national servicemen who were near the scene of the first Causeway strike when the second explosion occurred, apart from the civilians.

★

'The Malaysians have struck back. I take it the reply is already being delivered?' Chong said, trying hard to sound gung-ho, while he knew that the scenario had changed in a very profound way.

His new Mindef liaison officer for the day, Major General Tommy Tan, answered, 'Yes, sir. The flight time is hardly twenty minutes. Kuantan and Subang are under attack,' and he looked at his watch, 'just about now.'

In that half hour, from the time the surface-to-surface missiles were fired from Seremban to the first sighting of the incoming Falcons, there had been frantic movements at the two air bases. The planes at Subang had all taken off and were in a holding pattern at 3,000 feet over Sumatra. The aircraft at Kuantan had all taken off and flown to Thailand. In their place were wood and cardboard creations, some actually had sagging wings from a sudden downpour a few hours earlier, insignificant detail for the fighter-bomber pilots who had discovered the enemy in their firing slots. Almost at the same time as the aircraft opened fire at Subang, swarms of anti-aircraft missiles from batteries hidden in rubber plantations rose into the angry sky. That was General Tan Sri Omar Burhanuddin's little surprise for General Peter Woo and his High Command. Eight of the first wave of F-18 Hornets were hit, the second wave of fourteen F-16 fighters veered off just in time but they still lost four aircraft. The story was repeated at Kuantan; the Singapore Air Force had lost another nine aircraft here, a total of twenty-one, a level of loss that Tan Sri Burhanuddin knew would be a little painful for General Woo to bear in a matter of minutes.

Chong, Dr Wong and General Woo knew now why the Malaysians had destroyed the Hawkeye despite the high risk of severe retaliation; not because it was a soft target to appease their wounded nationalism. More Hornets and F-16s were sent out to neutralise the missile batteries, then all the hangars, then the aircraft hiding out over Sumatra.

'They have to land in a Malaysian airport within forty-five minutes or so. Then we'll get them,' Major General Tommy Tan told the Prime Minister.

'Unless of course, they get permission to land in Sumatra.'

Singapore aircraft would not intrude into Indonesian air space in these circumstances. There was also the problem of the Malaysian aircraft that had flown to Thailand. They must have landed somewhere there.

★

Most of Kuala Lumpur and its dormitory towns of Petaling Jaya, Subang Jaya and Shah Alam had seen the fireworks around the old Subang International Airport, now given over to the RMAF; the screaming jets, the explosions, the fiery crashes. Not one pilot had been captured alive, in Subang or Kuantan.

★

Suleiman Bakri resisted the temptation to go on television to announce that a major air attack had been repulsed and that the Singapore Air Force had paid a high price. Instead, he called the Operations Room into session to announce the encouraging news, conveyed to him in some detail by a colonel he hadn't seen before. He was told to be prepared for bigger things as the full action was still unfolding. In the meantime it was considered essential that the Prime Minister and other key members of the Ops Room take extra precautions regarding their personal safety. Singapore was known to have Special Operations forces, similar to the British SAS.

It was now 8.30 a.m.; a new chapter was beginning within Singapore. Asma Latiff, Mohammed Ariff and Ah Ching had begun their mission. Ah Ching drove his Bedford north to Changi where he took the roundabout and headed back to the city. Mohammed Ariff drove south to Outram and Tiong Bahru where he took Kim Seng Road to Orchard Road. He parked in a back lane and went to the terrace of a building a little to the left of the Istana turn-off. He sat in the shade of the high wall and took out one of those bulky things that he smoked. It would be at least another twenty minutes before his colleagues were ready.

★

Nancy Lim, a short woman with a permanent pout and an earnest look, gave the telephone to the Prime Minister. Chong began with a neutral, 'Hello.'

'Yes, so what you got to say?'

Chong noticed the touch of Singlish or Manglish. He tried to maintain the informality: 'We got to talk. You know that. Don't be so aggro, lah.'

'What do you think your planes have been doing, ah? You want *sayang*, ah?' said Suleiman.

'You know we can't allow your planes any chance to come near Singapore. We took that action only because your missile attack showed that you don't want peace,' said Chong.

'You squat on my land and you want peace?'

'We are not squatting on your land. We have only taken what is ours, for our water. Only, it was not spelt out clearly in the documents when we left Malaysia.'

'You were kicked out of Malaysia. The Tunku only agreed to supply you with water on terms to be negotiated. There was no question of land,' said Suleiman.

'Look, we can talk this over and come to an agreement. But first we got to stop fighting. How about a ceasefire, or at least a cooling-off period. I am sure that you know that there are third parties interested in a peaceful settlement.'

'You think I can just whistle and all the fighting will stop or what? Let's talk again later.'

'Later, when?' asked Chong.

'After your men have gone back to your island. I suppose that is difficult in the circumstances. They all have to swim, eh?'

'There is no need to be sarcastic, Suleiman. I'm talking about stopping further bloodshed.'

Suleiman did not miss the omission of any honorific.

'No, Chong, that is not what you are talking about. You are trying to find a way to stop the fighting while you are still on my land. The fighting will stop when there is a return to the status quo, that is, your men on your island and my men on our land. Water is secondary.'

Chong realised his mistake in not calling him *Encik* (Mr) or Mr Prime Minister, but it was too late now.

'That's not true, water is the main thing.'

'For you, but for our fighting men every inch of Malaysia is precious. You are not going to get an inch, under whatever pretext,' stated Suleiman firmly.

'There's no point in prolonging this conversation.'

'Hey, you were the one who wanted to talk to me, remember?'

'I am always prepared to go the extra mile for peace.'

'Peace, my foot. Your planes are attacking Subang again.'

And he put down the phone.

Chong was clearly irritated at the direction their conversation had taken. It looked as if he was the one who needed peace more than Suleiman.

'If he touched my city, his twin towers would be twin disasters,' Chong told Dr Wong, who was by now leaning on his table with an anxious look and specks of sweat on his shiny face.

'I have been given the task of conveying some bad news,' he told Chong, scrutinising his face for any inkling of what his reaction might be.

Powerful men have been known to punish the messenger for bringing bad news. Not seeing any overt signs of irrational behaviour, he told Chong the whole news, in big bite: 'CK Tang's and the Raffles Centre have been bombed. There's been heavy casualties and widespread damage. Rescue teams have just reached the scene.'

Chapter Eleven

Asma Latiff had been asleep only a couple of hours when she was awakened by loud knocking on the door, apart from the chiming doorbell. She was in a state of total disorientation as she crept up to the door and asked softly, 'What?'

'*Saya*, lah.'

'Go away.'

'*Bukah*, lah.'

'Go away.'

'*Bukah*, lah.'

She opened the door; the neighbours might already have heard the sorry exchange. Mohammed Ariff stood at the door with a cheeky smile on his face. He had been unable to sleep, his life was speeding up to a climax in a very short time, it was all happening too fast. Asma need not have waited till this last moment to yield to him; he would have followed up the slightest encouragement, but she had always been very cold towards him. Only now had he been bold enough to take his chances, for there might not be a tomorrow for them. Every detail of their mission had been planned and tested; there had been three trial runs. But here now was the real thing. They might be the cause of huge human suffering; the thought bothered him. Asma had all the answers. Theirs was a pre-ordained duty, and they had been chosen by the will of God. Sex sealed their courage and commitment.

They got up at about 5 a.m. and Mohammed Ariff returned to his flat and Asma Latiff took a hot shower. She said her prayers, drank a glass of Ovaltine and ate two biscuits. At six sharp she left the flat and went downstairs. All around her there was hectic activity. Everybody, it seemed, wanted to go out at the same time. Mohammed Ariff came by in his car and gave her a lift to the farm. They parted without a word: each knew exactly what the drill was.

She walked briskly to the back of the farm and removed the plastic covering from the van and checked to see if the motor would start instantly. She let it run as she got into the back and put a CK Tangs overall over her clothes, with rubber shoes, a scarf around her head and designer shades. She paused a moment to take in the scene, then she backed out and turned towards the farm entrance, running over three kinds of vegetable patches. The gardener would do an excellent job covering up the tracks. She would drive west and eventually come down beside Goodwood Hotel, turn left and left again into the CK Tangs deliveries area. A spot at the far end, near the corner entrances, was the preferred location to leave the van.

She parked it, locked it, and went up to the workers loitering in the deliveries area, for it was too early for things to arrive. She smiled at them and walked briskly up the stairs, third door to the left, down the corridor, down the escalators and out of the building by a side door used by staff. She took the underpass across the road to the cinemas. One more test remained – could she remember the number? She punched the digits in her mobile phone and she said only one word to the man who answered it.

'Okay.'

Ah Ching had been in the shower almost at the same time as Asma was. Actually, all over Singapore people were in the shower or shaving and getting ready to go out. It was a funny sort of day with military operations and curfews and this veneer of unreal normality. Ah Ching made a cup of coffee, smoked a cigarette, then went back to the bedroom to contemplate the sleeping figure of the only girl he had ever felt anything for; he pulled the blanket off gently to admire her full form. Well, he had to go; he kissed his *chilli-padi* on a delicate spot, and he was at the door when he heard her, 'Bye bye, Queensland.'

His drill was to walk to the godown, pull on a Raffles Hotel overall kept in the Bedford, and drive the van north, slowly, without breaking any traffic regulations, take the roundabout at Changi Airport and head back into the city. He would park the van in front of the hotel, a little to the right of where the bellboys would be standing, lock it, and walk up to reception, ignoring the others completely.

He would tell reception that the bags were here, and he would wait for the passengers from Changi. He would then take the corridor to the side, a door to the left, down the stairs, to the end of another corridor, into the staff rest area, one more door to the smoking area outside, and another door to the lane behind. He would walk briskly towards Dhoby Ghaut and Serangoon Road. His last task was to call the number he had memorised, and tell the man who answered the phone one word: 'Okay.' None of the people who had seen Asmah or Ah Ching at the two sites would live long enough to tell.

Mohammed Ibrahim's task was to be in a certain position at a certain time, both flexible, depending on circumstances. He had found for himself a fairly quiet spot, on the empty terrace of a building near the Istana, or Presidential Palace. He would get two phone calls, and each caller would say just the one word. He would wait fifteen to twenty minutes, then punch a fourteen digit number followed by the hash key on his mobile phone. If he was anywhere near where he was supposed to be, he should hear the result. He would follow with another fourteen digit number and the hash key, and he should again hear the result. That was it. His job would be done.

It was eleven when he finally walked down the stairs of the building and into a chaotic street. There were people running in two directions, away from or towards, he could not say, the scene of the two explosions. There were police and fire brigade vehicles, ambulances, troop carriers, followed by police and marching soldiers. Mohammed Ariff joined one group of people running into a side lane and he managed to get to his car. He could not cross the central axis, now totally blocked, so he drove to River Valley Road and cut north in a wide arc, then in another wide arc to Geylang. It took him two hours. He knew Asma and Ah Ching would have got home long before him, for they were to leave the area quickly, before the roads became blocked.

It was only a matter of time before the electronic sleuths discovered the sequence of calls on the five mobile phones used in the operation and traced the owners, but they had left the island long ago and the present operators of the numbers had kept the thing alive by paying the bills on time. The addresses were PO boxes, arranged with great difficulty but perfectly secure and untraceable. Possession of any of the five phones would be the only link to the explosions. That last link, too, would be lost for ever before the day was over. There would be no contact between the three of them or anybody else on this matter for at least a few months. If at all, they would be contacted and given specific instructions to escape – if they wished. The only escape route would be into Malaysia, then settlement in some obscure corner without attracting attention. Ismail Sebi would see to that. But, of course, that was if they wished to leave. The option was theirs. They could always slip back into their normal lifestyles. The perfect crime? All three knew there was no such thing and all three would have to make arrangements to vanish into thin air. They needed to keep cool.

★

'That was a stab in the heart,' a grim-faced Chong remarked as the details began to reach the Blue Room.

The CK Tangs junction in Orchard Road and the Raffles at the other end in Bras Basah Road formed a central fulcrum that controlled the entire city centre. It was now frozen stiff with government and military vehicles, and all entry points had been closed for three crossroad distances before traffic could reach the area. Every van, lorry, bus and even station-wagons were being checked across the island. Offices had ceased functioning and people were being sent home in the anticipation of curfew. Astronomical figures of dead and wounded were being rumoured; telephone traffic was reaching critical levels and automatic shutdowns were in the offing.

'Can I speak to Chris…'
'Can I speak to Ah Hong…'
'Carol, please…'
'Can I leave a message, please…'
'Didn't she call home?'
'Where's Teng gone to?'

Rapidly, the world's first wired city received the terrible facts, and an Important Statement that a curfew was going into effect within two hours, about 2 p.m. All offices should shut down immediately and everyone would go home. More Important Statements followed, ordering all medical staff, including specialists, in and out of government service, to report for duty at the nearest hospital; blood donors were required in all groups; casualty lists would be posted on special websites as and when they became available; there was a telephone number to report anyone who had not come home for an hour after curfew began.

Singapore, in typical fashion, in an orderly and efficient manner, was coping with a kind of disaster it had never encountered before. The anxiety to find out about loved ones was overtaken by immediate duty; thousands of people, in and out of uniform, laboured at the fringes of the bomb sites, carrying away the dead and dying, clearing the rubbish and getting nearer to the core of the monstrous thing. Power had been switched off blacking out the whole area. Gas fires continued to blaze in several pockets although supply had been shut down. The road frontages of the two landmark buildings were completely missing. There was severe damage to nearby buildings. It was clear that it would take days, maybe even weeks, to clear the debris and check out the safety of the standing walls. What was it? Missile or bomb? Dropped from a plane? Unlikely, for no one had heard any planes and there had been nothing on the radar. A car bomb? The promiscuous nature of a car bomb's visitation of death and destruction was something you only read about in far away places. Like Beirut. And Oklahoma. And Belfast. Singapore suddenly received a double dose that would acutely test its confidence.

★

'I can bring down his twin towers, you know,' Chong remarked to Dr Wong, who was intently studying telephone traffic figures from the area covering a period an hour before and after the explosions.

'This is going to take forever, but we will find a suspicious pattern, I am sure,' Dr Wong said. 'Most targets you can think of in KL will be empty. I know how Ismail Sebi's mind works. We could cause immense financial damage, but very few casualties.

Our problem is that KL has such a mixed population that at least half of any list of casualties would be Chinese. Do we want to do that? We have considered the question in the past and the consensus was that it would be counter-productive. I say we stick to military targets. Terendak Camp in Malacca would be an ideal candidate, but I doubt if the Malaysians have been silly enough to leave anyone in an obvious military target. I wonder where they have moved their paratroop brigade. Really useless in tropical terrain.'

'It was not easy to order the immediate closure of the markets. The Stock Exchange says they will function as normal, and leave it to brokers and staff to make their own sleeping arrangements if the curfew is not lifted later so they can go home. The other markets are taking the same position and they are all working as per usual. What do you say?' asked Chong.

'I would agree with that position and suggest that we lift the curfew at 6 p.m. for two hours for that last group of people to go home. We need not announce this decision until 5 p.m. because I really think that everyone who can should be home by 2 p.m. There is a lot of work to be done and there might be more military action, and I don't think we want too many people in the city centre.'

Major General Tommy Tan approached.

'Mr Prime Minister, I have some tentative figures. They are pretty shocking.'

'I can take it, so give.'

'250 to 300 dead, 450 injured, 250 seriously,' said Tan.

Chong took an audible deep breath and said nothing. He knew that those figures meant that, win or lose, his position as Prime Minister would not last long. Politically, they were unacceptable figures and there would be a price to pay. More and more lives would be touched by the mounting casualties, at the front and in the city itself.

'This is unacceptable,' Chong told the police liaison officer for the day, Deputy Superintendent Yeo Shook Weng. 'The Special Branch must have some idea who these people are?'

'We're checking, sir. Everyone that we know of has been under surveillance since Thursday. These are new people in the game. We believe they are new arrivals from the normal flow of people and traffic between the two countries. If they are not, it raises the dangerous possibility that they are sleepers who have been activated. That means this thing was anticipated, possibly years ago, and the people and equipment put in place. We must anticipate other attempts, but we are very watchful and I am sure we can prevent further outrages,' said Yeo.

He omitted to say that some suspects were getting the third degree, with ministerial approval, one of the unfortunate facets of war when lives are at stake.

'I hope you're right. I want you to go into the list of people who underwent long periods of detention and see if that has contributed to this tragedy in any way. Has there been any payback? Like that other incident? I was given a distinct under-taking by the Special Branch that all possible revenge-seekers had been accounted for,' said Chong.

'Yes sir, that is right.'

He was right, of course; sons, daughters, fathers, mothers, brothers, sisters, uncles, cousins, and in-laws would all be scrutinised and kept under surveillance for a time after each detention, and given a clearance, or referral to other sections for further action. Ah Ching was a cousin twice removed of a particularly sad victim of bureaucratic and political obstinacy, removed once too far to attract police attention. He would be a subject of interest when the Special Branch widened their sphere of enquiry. Even in that eventuality, he was already clean and had nothing to fear, he thought.

★

Neither Tessy nor his guests, Dave Mitchell and Dom Thomas, left the flat that morning. Dave installed himself on the balcony with a laptop, satellite phone and an odd-shaped, army radio on which he was listening to all sorts of air traffic; some exchanges sounded like air to ground, some were definitely on the police band. It was a tense but lazy morning of idle chat and Rose's ad hoc lunch of tinned foods with noodles. Then Dom got on the phone to speak to his friends, and Tessy busied about the place helping Rose.

The first call, to Peng Ah Pat, found the man not home. He had gone to the hospital.

'Why?' Dom asked.

After some hesitation, a female voice said, 'His daughter Louise was injured in the Raffles bomb.'

'I'm so sorry to hear that. How badly? Can I help in any way?' asked Dom.

'I know you are his old friend. Thank you. They say she will recover, but in what condition we don't know. The government is doing everything they can.'

'You must be his wife? Well, tell Peng when you see him that I have offered to help in any way.'

He shouted to Tessy the bad news.

★

Raymond Choo, the bureaucrat, was in a celebratory mood, regardless.

'We've done it, man. The two bombs are a small sacrifice for what we've got in Johore,' he said, and invited them all to go over to his place at the first opportunity to have a few cold Anchors and talk of old times.

★

Rahmat Majid was happy to hear Dom's voice, but very quickly his tone changed.

'Look, man, you be careful. I have a bad feeling about all this.'

He wanted a meeting after things settled down. Of course, being Malay, he was not too happy to see the Chinese ascendancy in hiving off a piece of what he considered the Malay peninsula.

★

Larry Lim was the least troubled by the events. His money was safe – all cash deposits in London and Zurich. His properties were on five-year leases with multinationals. And there was a new photo spread of Lingling on the Internet. His loyal wife, Mei Swee, was making lunch. His children, a son studying in New Jersey and a married daughter settled in Sydney, were calling constantly. He could go and live anywhere if things became too hot in Singapore.

'Remember the Bukit Bintang days? I've got some records and I still play your *Laju, Laju, Mulala* song sometimes.'

'You're living in the past, man. In any case, it's called *Bangawan Solo*, I think,' said Dom.

'Yah, but why not live in the past, ah? We had some good times, didn't we?' suggested Larry.

'Sure. Probably the best years of my life.'

'When are we going to get together again, ah?'

'We've got to wait until there's some peace and quiet.'

'Okay. Keep in touch. I must see you before you leave.'

'Sure. I want to see you, too,' said Dom.

★

There was still no sign of Ching Quee. Then Tessy gave Dom the number of an old work mate. He punched in the number and a woman answered, 'Hello.'

'Hi. This is Dom Thomas. Can I speak to—'

'Aiyah, this is Lucy. You sound so different now.'

'Hello, Lucy. How is your old man?'

'He's okay, but don't let him catch you calling him old man. He still thinks he's a young man, and he's saying that he needs a young wife to stay healthy. Rude, ah? I heard about your wife, ah. So sorry lah.'

'Yes, that was a little difficult for me. I want to see Eng Leng before I leave,' said Dom.

'With all these things going on, difficult lah. And he's got so many things to do. You speak to him on the phone. We can meet next time ah?' suggested Lucy.

'If you say so. Can I speak to him now?' asked Dom.

'Aiyah, he just stepped out for a short walk. You know, we've been cooped up here with the curfew. I'll ask him to call you, okay.'

'All right. One sec, I'll give you my number. Goodbye for now.'

'Goodbye.'

When Dom had put down the phone Tessy said: 'So you can't see him and you didn't get to talk to him, right?'

'Yes, but how did you know that?'

'He was injured in an accident and his speech is a little slurred and I've also heard that he has a limp. It's called loss of face.'

Chapter Twelve

Deputy Defence Minister Saw Chee Keng, looking at the casualty and damage figures, was convinced that the price was still within acceptable limits for their land gains. He intended to express that opinion in his next update for the Prime Minister, despite his reservations regarding making subjective statements. As a parliamentary secretary some years ago he had narrowly escaped dismissal for making a cigar joke in the presence of an American diplomat at the height of the Clinton-Lewinsky scandal. The Tuas bridge was a write-off; it would cost a bit to pull it down, let alone put up another bridge. But another twenty-four hours and the Causeway would be fully operational; a pontoon bridge bypass already made the crossing possible for a limited number of vehicles. The aircraft losses were troubling; there would be more since the Malaysians appeared to have growing numbers of missiles, both in battery formations and in hand-held configurations. It was also missiles that damaged the bridges, but these were bigger, more powerful ones. There could be more surprises; none more so than the Raffles and CK Tangs explosions, but these were definitely not missiles, both were with explosives packed in vans.

The base templates of the vans had been found embedded in the concrete. They were old vehicles and untraceable. But Dr Wong had seen something in the logs of the telephone company. One mobile telephone in the Orchard Road area had received two calls, and a short time later two calls had gone out to other numbers. Nothing odd there; what was unusual was that each of the four calls had lasted about fifteen seconds. Too much of a coincidence. The telephone company had provided the Special Branch with the five telephone numbers involved and their last known owners. Therein lay the problem. All five had not been used for a long time, although the service had been retained and the minimum fee paid promptly.

Calls to the five numbers produced the odd situation of all five being out of service. Destroyed in the explosions? But investigators were convinced that the five numbers had a sinister connection, mainly because the telephone company could not put traceable names and addresses to them. All five had bills going to a PO Box address, and the person who leased the box was, again, unknown. It could be surmised that the first two calls were to give the go-ahead, and the last two for another go-ahead, or even part of the firing mechanism. If that was the case, they must also have used a combination number after the phone had been engaged. That would not show up in the logs.

'Now to check people movements,' Dr Wong told the police officer.

There had to be something somewhere; someone must have seen something, the surveillance cameras must have picked up something. The slow, laborious task of interviewing people was already being organised. First, an Important Statement seeking anyone who had seen anything unusual in the areas around the time of the explosion, even the most trivial.

The grim task of naming the dead would take some time, but a fair number of names had already been confirmed. The government intended to have a mass burial with common funeral services. Only eight bodies had been identified and these were released to their families so they could make their own funeral arrangements. The hospitals were struggling to cope with the tragedy, but the private sector had responded magnificently and in some cases these people were working round the clock in makeshift surroundings.

The city stayed quiet under curfew, with surveillance stepped up, especially outside the towering housing colonies where the casualty toll could be very high if another bomb outrage was perpetrated. However, Singapore's military commanders believed, and Chong and members of the Blue Room concurred, that the next round of the conflict would be in Johore.

'The Malaysians must be getting impatient to get to grips with our boys,' Chong remarked.

'Then we should expect that their air force will finally put in an appearance,' Dr Wong said.

'That may well lead to a defining moment. We have a few surprises of our own, you know.'

'You mean the F-117As and the others that came in two weeks ago?'

'Oh, you know about that.'

'Of course, I know. You are right, these new aircraft could be decisive. They can knock out anything the Malaysians have,' Wong affirmed.

'We are looking for the big missiles. They can't hide them forever. Shall I call Suleiman now? All our friends should have spoken to him by now.'

'Not yet, let him sweat on it a bit more. By the way, I have been asked to bring to your notice that one of our songwriters has come up with a lovely idea. There is this belief that every war has been marked by a song and that we should be floating something. Maybe it will catch on.'

'A song? A song to fight the war? You must be joking,' said Chong, surprised.

Dr Wong, in a whisper, said, 'No, Steven. It's all part of war.'

'Okay, if you say so.'

'It's called *Lilly Mei-Lin*, based on a Second World War hit called *Lili Marleen*. Nice melody, nice words.'

'You are joking. Hitler's *Lili Marleen* to do our fighting? This is unbelievable.'

'It's not Hitler's song, it just so happened that it was German and it became a hit with the troops. We as a government will not have anything to do with the new version. Let them compose it and the radio stations can start playing it. I have no doubt that it will catch on.'

'Can you hum it?' asked Chong.

'Better than that. Watch the screen.'

Wong nodded to a man standing near the VCR on the central podium; the lights dimmed and the screen flickered with an old movie. Someone had edited it and the movie began with a woman walking to a stage; a very beautiful woman, a few short bars from the orchestra and the camera focused on her face. The thunderous reception died down and she started singing, in German. Chong knew then why it had been a hit. A haunting yet spirited tune, and the subtitles spoke of the loneliness and the yearning and separation of war, mothers and sons, wives and husbands, sweethearts and lovers. Very neutral to the human condition.

'Yes, I agree with you. But I must see the words. I don't want them saying stupid things,' said Chong.

'You mean, the words must be deep and meaningful?' asked Wong.

'You don't want me to reply to that, but you know what I mean.'

'Pardon me, I didn't mean to be sarcastic. They say the war used to stop at precisely 8 p.m. Belgrade time when the local station broadcast *Lili Marleen*.'

'You are exaggerating, of course.'

'That's what I read somewhere, but that is not important.'

'There must be nothing to link us to this song. I am a little nervous about the Nazi connection,' mused Chong.

Nancy Lim approached Dr Wong.

'Guess what,' he told Chong, 'they've found an English version of the song on the Internet.'

He took a quick look and handed it to the Prime Minister.

Chong read the first verse, slowly, word by word, line by line, the punctilious man he was.

Outside the barracks,
By the corner light,
I'll always stand
And wait for you at night.
We will create a world for two,
I'll wait for you
The whole night through,
For you, Lili Marleen.

'I see, the soldier's song. Nothing ideological here. Yes, I think the right words could work for us. But I still don't want the government linked in any way to this business. Okay?'

'Yes, of course, I thought so too. I'll pass it on. But I have taken it upon myself to suggest that *Lilly Mei-Lin* could start with the words:

Under the moonlight
On the Mersing beach…

to be followed by mention of Johore in general, then to familiar names in Singapore to tie it all in. Just a suggestion.'

★

Dom noticed by about midday that Dave Mitchell's mood had changed. He offered to make lunch for everyone. He was going to use whatever there was in the pantry, and Rose was to step aside. Dave made pasta, using Chinese noodles, and he made the sauce with a mixture of tomato sauce and mayonnaise. There was some leftover chicken which he deboned and added to the sauce. The result was a passable pasta meal.

Tessy opened a bottle of wine and it turned out to be a very good meal indeed. Dave said, to no one in particular, that he planned to leave as soon as he could get a plane ticket. With the curfew it was becoming difficult. Dom asked him where he was going.

'If I can get to Hong Kong, there is a direct flight to Paris by the French airline,' Dave said. 'That will suit me fine. But I've got to get out of Singapore first.'

'Any problem with that?' asked Dom.

'No, none,' said Dave.

Dom got the feeling that Dave was holding back. He'd know soon enough. In the meantime, Dave was proving great company. He was cracking jokes, singing Mandarin songs, then a risqué version of *Waltzing Matilda* linking the swagman and the jumbuk and the farmer, followed by an offer to take everyone to dinner if they had the opportunity.

'Why're you so happy suddenly?' asked Dom.

'I thought we might as well have a good time,' replied Dave.

'You're not on the run or something, are you?'

'Oh no, nothing like that. Cross my heart. I'll tell you the whole story some day.'

Rose whispered to Tessy, 'Must be woman trouble. All these *ang-mohs* have the same problem.'

★

Nancy Lim approached the Prime Minister to inform him that Suleiman Bakri was calling, and Chong felt his own confidence rising as he picked up the phone. The ball was in Suleiman's court, and both parties knew that.

Without any civilities, Suleiman got to the point directly: 'Are you going to pull back or what?'

'What gave you that idea? We could make a few adjustments to the line of control and maybe we can even talk money, but the water catchment areas and their adjacent areas are not negotiable.'

'We can turn Singapore into the new Beirut, you know that. My generals will not agree to give up any land on the mainland.'

'That I leave to you. You have to persuade them that the only way to avoid further bloodshed is to agree to a peaceful settlement. Let's start talking first,' suggested Chong.

'You misunderstand me. I don't have a problem with my generals, because they and I are in total agreement on this point. You have to pull back, or the war will take a more serious turn,' warned Suleiman.

'We don't underestimate your capabilities, but we are confident that we can hold what we have; and we have the means to inflict on you the same level of pain that you might be tempted to visit upon us. We have not resorted to terrorist activities, and we don't have to. An appropriate response to the bombing outrages in the city will be considered if a peaceful settlement is not in the offing.'

'Are you threatening me?'

'I'm not, but you must face the facts. You might do us some damage, but we can live with that if our water is safe. The sooner we reach a settlement, the sooner we can get on to the job of reconstruction. Have you considered putting a cash value on the land that has come under Singapore control?'

'Typical. So you think a few ringgits will solve the problem?'

'There are other concessions we could make, but we have to start talking first. Let's call a ceasefire,' said Chong.

'I called you to give you a chance to pull back. I could have made the demand to your High Commissioner here, but I thought a direct approach would be better. So your answer is that you are not pulling back?' asked Suleiman.

'Yes and no. We could pull back a little, if that will solve the problem, but not all the way back across the Causeway. And we are prepared to make financial reparations.'

'Not good enough. Goodbye.'

Chong started to respond, but Suleiman had already put down the phone.

Dr Wong was beaming.

'The talk about money was great. I think we've got them thinking in the right direction. It's the paradigm shift thing.'

General Peter Woo was on the line to speak to the Prime Minister. The Malaysian build-up was continuing and their forces were lined up in loose formations about twenty kilometres north of the Mersing Line. The movement of missiles was the only motor traffic, the soldiers were all tramping through the jungle; some were carrying their light armour in pieces.

'We can nip this thing in the bud if you give us the word,' the General said.

'The members of the Blue Room and I are firm on that. They have to fire the first shot from now on, then you can proceed with your operations. This self-imposed ceasefire on our part is to give them the opportunity for a peaceful settlement. The rest is up to them,' said Chong.

'Yes, I understand that, but we are ready. The initial aircraft losses won't happen again, and the troops on the Mersing Line have been alerted to expect an attack at any moment. The little trouble we had on the Mersing beach has been sorted out. We lost a few men, but the Malaysian marines have all been rounded up, in the marshes to the south-east. There were only eight left. That sort of caper won't happen again because we have extensive thermal imaging in place now. The night holds no surprises for us any more. As I explained earlier, this attack happened because we were convinced the terrain made an attack unlikely. And as we anticipated, the attack failed miserably, although it did us some damage. There was no way they could follow-up.'

'Yes, I accept that, but I must caution you that we must not leave any loopholes. We must be ready for any eventuality.'

'We are, Mr Prime Minister. The members of the Blue Room can rest assured on that score. In case of renewed hostilities, we will open another direct Blue Light line to keep you informed.'

'Yes, thank you, general.'

The next twenty-four hours would be critical, Dr Wong remarked.

★

General Tan Sri Omar Burhanuddin believed that a few more hits within Singapore city would have a salutary effect, but Ismail Sebi was saying that he could organise only one more, and that it had become extremely risky with the curfew and the increased surveillance. The army could not organise a land offensive with sufficient punch to carry it right up to the water without adequate air cover. The general, a very pragmatic man who spoke little, was aware of the damage done to his navy and air force by the lack of training and exercise. Then there were the breakdowns and equipment failures. As always, in the end the army had to carry the can. It was going to be difficult, but it had to be done.

In the next few hours all the disparate groups now forming in Johore would coalesce into a single formation on the western slopes of the central hills and hit the Singaporeans with everything in one spot, a few miles west of Keluang. The attack was scheduled for 1 a.m. The air force would do what it could to draw away the Singapore fighters, so the ground attack could break through and race south. Singapore's soft troops would be no match for the Malaysians. Remember the Commonwealth Games in Kuala Lumpur? All the Golds that Malaysia won? Singapore didn't even win a tin medal. Even the Singapore flag planted on Everest was taken there by two Malaysian Chinese living in Singapore.

Physically, the Singaporeans could be stopped. But the technology and the aircraft they had was a troubling thing. The General was saying very little to his Prime Minister. He had been having disagreements with Suleiman Bakri and his predecessors for some years over the slashing of the military budget and the cutbacks in training and exercises. The General could not

138

understand how the RMAF came to acquire three totally incompatible makes of fighter aircraft that made repairs and maintenance unnecessarily difficult and costly. At the same time, the Singaporeans were being more pragmatic, and they were getting new and better aircraft and equipment and pumping more money into training and exercise.

The battle plan arrived at by consensus was fairly straightforward. The details were left to the component units and services to work out. Missiles, aircraft and ground armour would be used in conjunction with seasoned men of the Malay Regiment. It was not going to be easy; there would be heavy casualties. The towns and cities had to be alerted for the possibility of attack, for there would be replies in kind for what was planned for Singapore city.

They had three types of missiles, all American, the only military purchase in which the general had become personally involved; put together in a hurry with the help of a Sri Lankan businessman who had contacts in the Pentagon. There were the surface-to-surface, new generation missiles that provided greater accuracy; the short-haul anti-aircraft batteries to protect the air bases, and the long-distance surface-to-air missiles to knock down aircraft at greater distances. These last had not been used yet; Tan Sri Burhanuddin was holding them back to give General Woo another surprise. The real secret of missile warfare was in electronics, and the *Truman* out in the South China Sea could determine the success or failure of equipment because of its considerable arsenal in electronic warfare. Military equipment had always had a problem with civilian overlap of their radio frequencies. Mobile phones were a real menace to missile guidance systems. The new missiles came with a guarantee that not only would they hit their targets but that counter measures would be futile. An expensive deal but worth it, the General was sure. It takes two to *joget*. They could indeed give the Singaporeans a bloody nose.

*

Captain Tan Howe Liang with Sergeant Silva, two other full-timers and the eight national servicemen that constituted the platoon had no idea that they were right in the eye of the storm, except that in this storm the eye bore the brunt of the fury. They had eaten satay and *bubur char-char*, a hot porridge sort of thing, from the hawkers before they had been driven away by the Military Police. By about eleven at night headquarters had begun alerting the entrenched troops of movements in the distance. Captain Tan's telephone rang every half-hour and each time the opposing forces were coming closer together in a direct line opposite his position.

'Doesn't look good for us,' he remarked to his sergeant. 'We must be in their sights. If their attack is going to be concentrated on us, there will not be much point in firing back. They will be using heavy guns. I don't know why our air force is letting them get into position. If it's an arrow-attack and we are at the point, I'm afraid Plan B will be in operation, and I don't need clearance for that.'

'If that's the case, I suggest we move east of the hills, because of the marshes to the south-east. Those guys to the east of us will have to move with us or they're goners,' said Silva.

'Yes, bend like bamboo and we won't break. Let the buggers through and we will spring the trap shut behind them.'

The sergeant was given permission to walk across to the platoons on either side to brief their commanders of the likely course of events. And they could brief their neighbours, but nothing was to be said on the telephone, for there was heavy tapping, by both sides. Of course, the initiative was with each commander to do what he thought was the best course to take when the action began.

*

At 1 p.m., without warning, the curfew was lifted in Singapore. The Important Statement also said that all auto-tellers had been topped up and withdrawals up to the usual limits were permitted, provided that there were funds in the accounts being used. It was about the same time that Ambassador Johnson issued a general directive to all Americans to leave the island any way they could. British, Australian, New Zealand, Japanese and other diplomatic representatives issued similar instructions shortly thereafter. People were being contacted by telephone and through social and professional networks, because Singapore television, radio and newspapers refused to carry the pessimistic orders.

The Malaysian High Commission was closed and the High Commissioner and his staff and their friends and families had hired a small cruiser to sail to Indonesia. It was also around midday that Changi Airport finally closed and all incoming aircraft were given notice that they would be allowed to land, at their own peril, but there were no refuelling facilities and they would not be allowed to take off again.

There was now a rush on the harbour. All sorts of small craft were in demand for the short run to Indonesian ports. Peter and Connie Chapman, David and Leslie Russell, and Ossie and Patricia Eisenberg managed to get on to a motorised sampan just big enough for all them to squeeze into.

'Make sure of your bearings at all times,' Peter told David, who being an Australian was familiar with the sea and sailing.

Fortunately, they were not alone. Their little sampan was just one among scores leaving the harbour in a generally southerly direction. Diplomats of many countries were availing themselves of Johnson's offer of a helicopter ride to the *Truman* to wait there for the duration. Four Chinooks got on to the task and moved about 180 people to the *Truman* by nightfall. Among them, Cohen and Janet. But all this time Dave Mitchell sat tight; he made no attempt to go to an auto-teller to take any money or to go to the harbour to seek a way out. And again without warning, an Important Statement at 4 p.m. announced that the curfew would be reimposed at 6 p.m. Curfew breakers faced the prospect of getting shot. Dave Mitchell said to no one in particular, 'Things are happening, or are about to.'

Chapter Thirteen

At Suleiman Bakri's request, General Tan Sri Omar Burhanuddin agreed to appoint a new liaison officer to the Ops Room, and promised to keep them all informed of developments at all times. He was cagey about times and forces, but he had given an indication that tonight was the night. That was good enough for Suleiman who had the full Ops Room in session by about 6 p.m.

At the last minute, on Ismail Sebi's advice, they moved to the Prime Minister's own bunker deep inside his official residence. It was as big as the Ops Room and the communications layout and facilities were first-rate. It looked as though it had been prepared for just such an occasion. It was feared that Singapore fighter-bombers would attempt what is known in the business of war as a decapitation, the removal of a country's leaders in one blow. It was as a precaution against such an eventuality that Singapore had its Blue Room deep underground with tonnes of granite for a roof.

*

The Malaysian commander was looking at what sort of ultimate settlement he might achieve, even as his forces were getting into position and the strategy of engagement was being put in place. The Singaporeans were determined to keep the water; there was no certainty that the Malaysians would be able to throw them back over the Causeway without control of the air; a confusing and confounding engagement of rapidly shifting fronts would work in Malaysia's favour, but there might not be much left of its own air force and navy. There would be heavy casualties on both sides because the national servicemen that Singapore was throwing into battle were going to be decimated. Irresistible force meets immovable object. An unhappy balance of death and injury; therefore, it was advisable to look at what sort of final settlement one might hope for.

Unbeknown to Suleiman Bakri and the Ops Room, the general had five possible conclusions on his table. The most feasible appeared to be that of selling the land that Singapore wanted. In any case, this was largely unproductive marshland. A neat, curving line could be drawn from the shore encompassing the areas critical to Singapore's requirements, cutting Johore Bahru. The land and sea to the east would go under Singapore control; this meant Malaysia losing some acreage under rubber and oil palm, and a fair bit of urban property in and around Johore Bahru. Singapore would gain a further advantage in addition to the Pasir Gudang port facilities – that bit of extra air space would mean that aircraft would be able to take off and land at Tengah Air Base without encroaching into Malaysian airspace.

'We can make them pay dearly for all this,' the General told his adjutant, Major Dollah Ahmad. 'But we must have strict parameters on what we may yield. What I have mentioned is the absolute limit.'

His main intellectual guide and confidante, Datuk Rahman Malik, the respected Professor of Asian and Oriental Studies, had helped the army's own strategic planning section in looking at the alternatives; and he too supported the so-called Water Line as an acceptable conclusion, if the money was right.

'But before we come to that,' the Datuk had said, 'we must give Singapore a good fight. We have to redeem our honour, then we will talk. Otherwise we will only be leaving behind unfinished business that could cause another war in the future,' he told the General on the secure phone. 'But in the process we are also going to set limits on Singapore's rearmament. There is no saying what they might do in the future if they again built up some muscle. They might want a bit more of Johore.'

'That means the United Nations and the Americans, and I don't know who else, will be drawn in to keep the peace and verify their compliance on armament levels. And who is going to determine what that level should be?' asked Tan Sri Omar.

'Any talks are going to be long and complicated. I would suggest that what that Australian Major said in his proposal has merit,' said the Datuk.

'I was thinking the same thing. We may be overreaching our-selves if we seek Singapore's defeat. Pushing their men east against the marshes, sealing off escape across the water by repeated destruction of the Causeway and concentrated fire on anything on the water would bring about the desired effect. There is just so much you can do from the air when there is heavy movement by both sides on the ground.'

'I take it to mean that we stick to the first part of the agreed plan, and make the desired changes once battle is joined?' queried the Datuk.

'Yes.'

With that, Major Dollah Ahmad, who had been listening in, started writing down the moves and commands he thought were necessary to achieve what his general had agreed to.

But first, battle had to be joined.

*

It was a typical steamy night in Singapore. The air-conditioners were working full blast, but still tempers flared easily. Fear for loved ones in Johore mixed with exhilarating thoughts of what a greater Singapore could achieve. There were greater opportuni-ties, even a higher standard of living, the spread of skyscrapers across the Causeway, and there would be scores of new bridges like in Hong Kong, or even Manhattan. The impossible dream was coming within their grasp.

It was Steven Chong who had first mooted the idea of actually going to war to secure Singapore's water supplies. He had done so not in public, but in a keynote address to members of the Blue Room shortly after he became Prime Minister. His gut feeling was that the idea would not be opposed by the average Singaporean, the so-called HDB Heartlander.

The words that had sparked the critical chain of events leading to this night of high drama were being replayed on the Blue Room screen. He looked much younger here and his speech seemed to have greater conviction than any others he had made since then. Chong, too, was in the chamber to be reminded where and how it all began.

My friends, my fellow Singaporeans, my compatriots, I have given long thought and I have consulted many of our best intellects to come before you with this suggestion. It appears to me that events in Malaysia, the regional environment, and our own circumstances are all fast approaching a point that occurs only once in a blue moon for us to seize our opportunities. I am talking about securing our water supply. I don't have to remind you that water has been a constant source of anxiety for our people and it has placed a brake on our planning for the future. Hong Kong without its New Territories was always a lost cause, but Singapore on its own has still managed to get along pretty well. Now think how great Singapore could be if we, too, had our New Territories? I can paint you a magnificent vista of a great spread of skyscrapers right into Johore, plenty of land for industry, sufficient backbone for the creation of a great financial centre, but, most importantly, we will be masters of our own destiny. Water is the key, and I suggest we go out and get it while we have the opportunity.

Applause, muted by concern at the suggestion of war.

Steven Chong noticed the reserve, and continued:

When our forefathers landed on these shores, many of them had only the clothes on their back. But they worked hard and built businesses that now cover all of South-East Asia in a network of mutually beneficial enterprises. Their dreams and hard work will all come to nought if we allow the Malaysians to determine the limits of our growth and influence. All the great heroes of legend and history will be with us when we embark on this great adventure. The Singapore Lion has to roar, it cannot remain a sheep to be pushed and shoved at the whims of any zealot who happens to come along across the Causeway. We have endured so many insults and provocations, yet we have not lost our patience or our temper. Our language has always been temperate and accommodating, but all this has been taken as a weakness. The Singapore Lion is quite capable of looking after itself. The Lion has to roar. The time has come.

The video captured louder applause, and some roaring sounds. Steven Chong knew then that he was on his way.

I am inviting each one of you to join me in embarking on an

enterprise that is bold and breathtaking, a typically Singaporean enterprise that promises a lasting solution to our problems while at the same time bestowing great honour on ourselves. The Singaporean will walk tall in the world, with a new-found respect of the Super Powers. We have the potential to be one of the centres of the great financial and business transformation that is happening in this millennium. I would like to call it the Singapore Millennium. We are in the right place at the right time to take charge of Asia's evolving discovery of itself. We hold no anger or prejudice against anyone. We will continue with our regionalisation and globalisation. The Singapore Lion is on the move. But to begin with, all we want is the water that we are entitled to. So let us rise to the occasion and seize our opportunities. Our forefathers will smile on us and our descendants will marvel at our boldness. So roar with me and let us march together into this golden future.

The recorded roars were then joined by loud cheering and roars from the live audience. Steven Chong looked around; yes, the same faces except for the military representatives. Bright, shining faces reflecting the new determination.

Dr Wong approached the Prime Minister and Chong noticed the man's misty eyes.

'The blue moon has come, Steven,' he whispered.

'Yes, I know. There are many possibilities, you know. The strategy-people have come up with three more likely scenarios. I don't know what to believe. The die is cast. Pardon the mixed metaphors: may the chips fall where they may, let the cookie crumble whichever way.'

'Keep your cool, Steven. You sound nervous. This is not the time for it.'

Chong said with a laugh: 'You are right, but believe me, I am not nervous. I have absolute faith that by morning the situation will be that we have substantially achieved our aims.'

'Substantially?'

'You never believed that we will win everything, did you? This is not an all or nothing business. We can only hope to achieve the core things, and that is the water, the catchment areas, the pumping station and the route of the pipes. I think we will achieve that. It is the cost that worries me. A price has to be paid,

146

and we have sent in our young men to pay it in blood. That has been a haunting thought for me the last few days.'

Dr Wong was intensely aware that Chong's eldest son was over there somewhere. There had been a security blackout on the boy's exact location, but he was believed to be with an artillery unit some distance back from the front. And Chong had suffered the family trauma of an uncle seriously injured in the CK Tangs explosion. He was in intensive care and unlikely to recover. The Prime Minister was also paying a price.

★

People were glued to the Internet and the television, which was showing old Chinese movies, Roy Rogers westerns and discontinued quiz shows, but Channel 5 was the universal choice because it appeared to be the preferred channel for Important Statements. The first English version would be followed by other language translations. Apart from that, television was a total bore, but the Internet was where the action was, information and misinformation, insults, twisted history, racial and religious jokes, constant warnings from the thought-police that action would be taken against rumour-mongers and purveyors of racial and religious hate.

But Singapore's official reach on the Internet had its limits. AprilMay was back to suggest that KL's precious twin towers would be twin disasters before sunrise. AzlanMalik said Singaporeans might have water to drink for a few days, but they wouldn't be allowed to wash their backsides. Keep your thoughts above the navel, HotShot suggested. *AyamKecil* (Small Chicken) said Singapore would sink under its own poo. That's Johore Bahru's problem right now, HotShot said, for part of the arrangements had been that Singapore provided treated water for JB. Now that had been cut, by the Malaysians; a classic case of cutting the nose to spite the face. MatSalleh came back with, How did they like a touch of Beirut? SuzieWong replied that terrorists would get their just desserts in due course; the net was closing on them. Prostitutes please keep out of this conversation, AzlanMalik said. She's too good for the likes of you, AprilMay countered.

Twenty dollah? asked *AyamKecil*. Better that twenty ringgit, AprilMay suggested. And so on.

In all this inane traffic the only bit of news of any significance was that KL's diplomatic and foreign community and the rich and famous had also left the capital, in the same way as had happened in Singapore. Not news to members of the Blue Room, but certainly so elsewhere in the island, for now the realisation came that the war could indeed come close to home.

*

The sleeping arrangements on the *Truman* left a lot to be desired, if you were a couple, for the skipper was a cunning old fox. The men and women were given bunks on different decks, separated by a twenty minute walk down narrow corridors and stairs. There were no children on board, the last lot having flown out of Singapore the previous day.

Janet Lim's enthusiasm for the carrier evaporated pretty quickly, but it was all too late to change. There was no going back to Singapore for at least three days, she had been told. And Janet had to be especially careful where she went and who she spoke to, for there were only four non-Caucasians among the women.

She found a kindred spirit in Michelle Martin, third-generation Chinese from Montreal whose husband was an information secretary in the Canadian embassy. Together they set about finding out everything they could about the *Truman*, to pass the time, although one of the dining areas had been converted into a lounge with a stereo and satellite TV for their use.

The first thing they learned was that the *Truman* was so big it was difficult for the human mind to comprehend the astronomical figures. It had 2,000 kilometres of wiring to light 30,000 lights, three kitchens to serve 18,150 meals a day and the stores stocked enough food to fill seven supermarkets. Then there were the 14,000 pillowcases and 28,000 bedsheets for the bunks and 140,000 rolls of toilet paper to be distributed every day. Provisions include 1.5 million sheets of writing paper and 600,000 ballpoint pens, and there were 2,000 telephones. A big ship. A very big ship, Janet and Michelle agreed. But then again, dwarfed by the next carrier to enter service, the *USS Ronald Regan*.

★

The shifting, self-serving positions that accompany linguistic gymnastics at the United Nations are always a sight to behold, except that the world has no time for speeches and all news is down to a few seconds of sound bites, accompanied by pictures if one is lucky enough. In a world overflowing with action footage, a UN speaker stands no chance of being heard in the world at large, except as part of some other story in a news magazine.

Singapore needed its message to be carried through to the decision-makers of the world. To that extent, Singapore had chosen a list of emotive words and imagery, like *ethnic cleansing*, *religious extremists*, *terrorist car bombs*, the *right to a water supply* (likened to the right to breathe the air), and *ceasefire* and *peace talks*. It all sounded so reasonable. Malaysia, on the other hand, pushed the idea that naked aggression should never be rewarded, that Singapore had no pre-ordained right to Malaysia's water, the invaders must immediately pull back to their side of the Causeway. Malaysia's peaceful intentions were evident in the fact that it had never cut the water supply, in spite of Singapore's unfriendly acts and provocations over a long period of time.

The aggrieved victim had a case. The Islamic media would love it. If Saddam and Iraq were punished so brutally for the Kuwait invasion, what should be done to Singapore for its affront to civilised co-existence?

The Indonesian contribution was an elegant discourse on the need for peaceful consultation to take the place of armed conflict, but in the end it was a slight tilt in Malaysia's favour. Only just, Chong concluded back in the Blue Room. Thailand and the Philippines were fairly neutral in their speeches. Britain, Australia and New Zealand, all partners in the moribund Five-Nation Security Arrangement with Malaysia and Singapore, abstained from speaking at all. The cake was still in the oven, as it were; wait a while longer before deciding the rights or wrongs.

★

Palembang had never seen anything like it. The sudden arrival of all these well-heeled tourists had led to an acute shortage of hotel rooms, and now fully-furnished private homes were on offer if the rent was right. The restaurants were having a boom time, the insistence on imported bottled water notwithstanding. Night markets bloomed with new merchandise; money in circulation always did miracles for the local economy, and President Othman liked the minor boom the area was experiencing. Every cloud has a silver lining.

As night settled on a carnival-like Palembang, Singapore decided to switch off all its public lighting and an Important Statement urged people to switch off all outside lights and to observe a blackout for the duration. KL followed suit soon after. The small towns in Singapore's control in Johore had no choice, KL had simply switched off their section of the national power grid. But nothing was going to stop the hawkers, they were back at the front, with the hot noodles and satay and the *bubur char-char*, the fruit juice and the *ice-kacang*, closely followed by the 'twenty dollah' girls.

Brigadier General Soh Huck Cheng was in despair as he saw the smoke of cooking fires rise behind his lines. There were lights of all descriptions, the hum of humanity hard at work with an overlay of thousands of assorted hi-fi equipment playing all manner of music. He even thought he heard *Love Is A Many Splendor'd Thing*. What, *Summer Holiday*? *Good music never really dies*, the General told himself. Good music? *More like fossils*, he corrected himself.

He had managed to keep this opportunistic mob a good 200 metres away from his men, but he was given to understand that business was still brisk. Before long, he would retreat to his field headquarters south of Jemaluang and await the surprises of the night, as he had been promised by Headquarters.

★

For Jaffar Ibrahim, it was like a second honeymoon, for there was no way Stella could go back to Singapore. So they stayed together in the love nest, but the problem was that there was no food in the house. It took all of Jaffar's clout to put together a decent pantry – and get two cases of bottled water. There was no power, so there was no television. Candles were romantic. Stella and Jaffar wondered how the war would go; should they try to make it back to Singapore if they had the chance, or should they stay on and see what opportunities the new land offered? They were now becoming a close twosome, and they were also thinking as a couple. Circumstances were driving them closer together. Stella wondered if she would have to take a Muslim name.

Chapter Fourteen

Dave Mitchell informed the Texeira household about lunchtime that the war was not going too well for Singapore. There had been heavy casualties on the ground, many aircraft had been lost and the first Mersing Line had been abandoned for the second line of defence, Mersing south to Kota Tinggi, west to Kulai and Pontian Kecil on the Straits of Malacca. He had been listening to a whole range of radio traffic, occasionally interrupted by long screeches and an unfamiliar *blip*, *blip*, *blip* which he assumed were bursts of data transmission. Very sophisticated stuff, if they could cut right in and do their work as and when they wished. Probably Singaporeans at work, for only they had the technological nous for that sort of thing in the region. Unless, of course, the *Truman* had something to do with it. The Americans were probably the supreme practitioners of electronic warfare, but if they had a hand here they were not being neutral. What game were they playing?

★

The members of the Blue Room listened and watched grimly as the battle reports streamed in, with occasional graphics on the large screen. Chong's face became even more set in a scowl as he grilled the air force liaison officer for an explanation of why their fighters had been so vulnerable. Colonel David Lim was sweating as he realised that all eyes were on him; he could only repeat that the technical section was checking pilot reports and trying to figure out the reason.

While considerable damage had been done to the Malaysian attackers on the ground, the RSAF had been unable to stop them. Missiles were held responsible for almost all of Singapore's aircraft losses, while the attacks on the missile batteries and launchers themselves had not been as effective as anticipated. Some RSAF aircraft were brought down far out in the South

China Sea as they sought to launch long-distance, stand-off, Cruise-type weapons.

The technical section was beginning to suspect a superior electronic source at work. When the Colonel passed this piece of conjecture to the Prime Minister, he was met with a few choice expletives. Chong seemed to be struggling with himself as he made his way to the podium and paused as an aide adjusted the mike and switched it on.

'The bloody Americans have done it to us, I have no doubt about that,' he said, as Dr Wong realised that the *bloody* was a sure sign that the man was rattled. 'For years they have been trying to sell us their shonky anti-missile systems. Now they are providing us the reason why we should have bought the blasted system. If this is what I think it is, this is electronic warfare, and the Americans are taking sides. That's why the *Truman* has come here. How will they react if they begin to suspect that their precious carrier has become a legitimate target? Dr Wong, have a word with your Beijing contact. We need an immediate intervention of some sort. Otherwise there's no telling where this war will take us.

'Gentlemen, there is another side to the story. The fact that we have had to take a step back to the second line of defence is not a retreat. Bend like a bamboo, and all that. We remain committed to the original target of retaining the water resources. There will be many stories emanating from the war zone, some good, some bad, but I must urge you to keep your cool and hold steady to the task ahead. I am afraid that there might even be personal losses, but consider that as a noble sacrifice for the greater good. Look at it this way, we still control all that land from Pontian Kecil to Kulai and Kota Tinggi and north up to Mersing. That includes our freshwater resources. And we are going to hold that line.'

★

Backtracking to where and when the great battle began, it was about 1 a.m. when the first shot in the Malaysian offensive was fired, and that was a single missile that rose from the trees around Seremban and streaked in a low trajectory to hit the Causeway with pinpoint accuracy. This time the destruction was widespread, for even the temporary pontoon constructed some distance away was blown out of the water. The helicopters had picked up the incoming missile too late for their own missiles to be used against it.

Singapore's reply was both instantaneous and powerful. Waves of aircraft took off from Tengah and Sembawang and two other hitherto unknown locations in the west of the island, zeroing in on what was left of the Subang and Kuantan bases. One group concentrated on the rubber and oil-palm estates around Seremban looking for missile launchers, another group cruised the Straits waiting to pounce on any threat from Malaysian aircraft known to be in Sumatra; another group cruised the east coast of the peninsula in case the Malaysian aircraft that had been taken north put in an appearance.

The F-18 Falcons were given the crucial mission of neutralising the Malaysian ground offensive, and they suffered the heaviest losses to missile attacks, allowing the Malay Regiment to slice into Singapore lines.

Dave Mitchell, listening to frontline radio and telephone conversations, knew that Singapore's national servicemen were about to learn some painful facts about war. *Saving Private Ryan* was great to see on screen, but this was the reality. Real blood, real pain, real death.

Captain Tan Howe Liang had no hesitation in moving his men to the right flank when the attack came. As he had anticipated, it began with rocket and grenade attacks on the concrete barriers while he and his men hugged the ground some distance away. They rolled on the ground and crawled as enemy fire intensified; and the Captain believed that the first Malaysian soldiers would be leaping over what remained of the barriers at any moment. But he and his men would keep on moving and desist from firing rather than give their position away. While it was an act of self-preservation, the tactic spread confusion in the enemy. Were they walking into a trap? The offensive slowed, while in the air the other battle flared. Screaming aircraft and missiles, flashes of infra-red cutting across flaming crashes and low thuds of ground hits. Cannon and mortar fire lit up the night, but the realisation that the Malay Regiment was inside their lines silenced most of Singapore's big guns further south; only those pre-targeted on points north of the lines could keep firing. There was now confusion as to where the front was, who and where the enemy was.

This cut both ways as groups of men wheeled and turned. The confusion this created among the Singaporeans forced their High Command to order a fan-like retreat, greater in the west and sticking close to Mersing in the east. It somewhat resembled the second line of defence, but High Command declined to call it that.

'At least that will cut down on casualties by friendly fire,' General Woo commented, talking to the Prime Minister on the phone. 'But I need a good explanation as to why the RSAF has not been as effective as we had expected it to be. Super aircraft with intelligent, fit and extremely well-trained crews. So I want to know what happened.'

'Has the technical section spoken to you?' asked Chong.

'Yes, they are talking about electronic warfare. The Malaysians can't run a telephone system, let alone wage electronic war. I doubt the *Truman* would intervene in this manner,' said Woo.

'I wouldn't put it past the Americans. They tried to sell us that anti-missile system and we declined, remember?'

'Yes, but instead of that we bought all those expensive planes from them.'

'I think they were more anxious to sell us the anti-missile system. It doesn't seem to be moving well. The Falcons, well, everyone wants them,' Chong stated.

'If your conclusions are correct, then the Americans may have opened a whole new can of worms here.'

'Yes, I am afraid so, but we are looking at other avenues to even the playing field.'

'Like?' asked Woo.

'Soon, I will tell you soon. Can't tell you now,' fudged Chong.

'If there are other strategic or security considerations, I'd like to know soonest.'

'You will, General. You will. Goodbye.'

The second line was holding, but both sides were regrouping

and fighting could resume at any moment. That was the status report that Captain Tan Howe Liang received. He was already a hero to his men for having taken the brilliant action to get out of the way of a superior force. His fear was that he was near the northernmost point of the line: he stood a good chance of getting cut off. His line of retreat was narrow with the river and the beach at his back and marshes to the right. If a strategic move to the rear, or retreat, became necessary he and his men might not be able to move down fast enough. The beach appeared to be the best way out, but it was a dead end without boats. *How apt*, he thought, *dead end*.

There were about seventy to eighty other men at this point, all becoming squeezed. He thought it was time that he took his men away from the crush and requested permission to do so. No, he was not to move, others might also get the same idea. So the Captain and his men stayed where they were, wondering what their next move should be. They still had most of their ammunition, because they had not known where to fire once the Malay Regiment had gone past them. They held fire and waited, and moved on. But they were all still alive.

The Captain knew that he would have to explain why that was, since the position held by his platoon had been the focus of the offensive. He would think up some good excuses, he might even break up his platoon and mix them up with other groups, to indicate the confusion that surrounded them at the time. In any case, everyone would be asking about the RSAF. What happened to them? They were expected to pound the enemy into the ground while the men behind the lines watched. Things hadn't worked out that way; they never did in war. He must at least use up most of the ammunition, to indicate that they had put up a fight. So the marshes and the mangrove swamps to the north got a pasting.

'I don't think the crabs have ever seen anything like this,' Sergeant Silva told the Captain.

'Yes, and the leeches and the bugs and the mosquitoes,' the Captain said as he opened up with the machine-gun.

A Dunkirk-style sea lift from the Mersing beaches would be too much to hope for, so he should plan to move quickly, the

Captain told his Sergeant. Failing that, they must make their getaway in the boats they could find in the river.

A captain from another platoon came over and they discussed the situation. Captain Tan never let on that he had a last ditch plan of escape if they became trapped. *We save ourselves first; these other guys can look after themselves.*

An upshot of this firing was that the Singapore High Command believed another offensive was coming through the swamps and sent in the helicopter gunships for close-in attack. A mistake, without the Hawkeye, for they came into the gunsights of three Harriers, which had come up hugging the coastline close to the ground, remaining unseen on radar.

The control room of the *Truman* knew what was happening, but declined to alert the Singaporeans this time, condemning the helicopter crews.

Captain Tan saw the Harriers come into view and his sergeant finally got to use the anti-aircraft rocket launcher he had been carrying for most of the previous twenty-four hours. All three Singapore helicopters were hit simultaneously and went down in flames, but Captain Tan and his men had the thrill of seeing their rocket bring down one of the Harriers.

'Note that down in your little book, Sergeant,' Captain Tan said. 'Time, place, aircraft and result. Crashed in flames.'

Singapore still had control of the air, despite occasional missile attacks, but the pilots were flying in haphazard formations and successfully eluding the missiles by relying on their own eyes. They were thus able to hit back on the ground almost immediately. Odd, their radar lock-on warning devices were not working, but the missiles were still not getting the upper hand.

On the ground the line had become settled again, but this time there were no concrete barriers; the troops had to dig into the ground and use whatever was at hand for cover and shelter. That was where their training would come into play. Their lives could depend on how effective they were. But the advantage was that while the aircraft stayed clear of the frontline showing their respect for the missiles, the big guns that Singapore had installed further back were now coming into full play.

Free fire, quick and blinding and deafening.

'The Malay Regiment would be having a difficult time,' Chong remarked to Dr Wong.

If Singapore had suffered casualties in the retreat, the Malaysian forces were suffering in the standstill. They would have to move, and quickly, either forward or backward.

★

Tan Sri Omar called his Prime Minister and suggested that a temporary truce be arranged.

'Either in the next offensive I try and go all the way and clear these fellows right out, or there will be a stalemate that will not be to our advantage,' he told Suleiman Bakri. 'So it would be a good idea to spend some time talking. It will also give you an idea what's on their minds. Also, I would like you to have a talk with Datuk Rahman Malik, the Professor. He has some useful ideas.'

Suleiman Bakri was initially outraged by the Professor's suggestion.

'We will have to settle for the money, because I don't think Singapore is going to give up the water thing,' he told the Prime Minister. 'We can do the Beirut thing to their city, but we must expect replies in kind.'

'But the Americans will not allow aggression to succeed. They will continue to help us, and that should tilt the balance in our favour on the battle field,' said Suleiman.

'The Americans will abandon us the moment they see some advantage on the other side. They are not to be trusted,' suggested the Datuk.

'I don't want to approach Steven Chong with a ceasefire proposal. That will be a sign of weakness. Why don't you call your friend Dr Wong and make the suggestion as if it came from you? And you will have to be quick about it.'

'Right away, Tuan Perdana Mentri.'

★

The mood in the Blue Room improved marginally from utter desolation to plain desolation with the new reports from the front. Singapore's big guns were having a field day, but the grim reality was that Singapore's own casualty figures remained high, on the ground and in the air. The navy could not be usefully deployed other than to guard the waters in the south, but it was a well-trained and highly efficient little unit that was on standby for greater things.

Captain Tan Howe Liang was thinking the same thing, that the navy could pluck them to safety. But getting to the big navy vessels was tricky; he would have to use the small craft tied up on the river bank at Mersing. So who was going to return the boats to the locals? He might have to find their owners and get them to do the ferrying, or the boats would have to be abandoned at sea.

Sergeant Silva took two NS men with him and went into Mersing to locate the various boat owners when the Captain explained to him the likely course of events. They would be prepared when the time came.

★

Inspector Michael Rodrigues had been looking at surveillance film taken from buildings throughout the Orchard Road area and he had seen nothing suspicious. The cinema complex on the other side of the road from the CK Tangs site had been extensively damaged, but fortunately the cinemas had been closed at the time although the lobby was open. The film from the surveillance camera inside the building had been collected and brought along with all the others, and the inspector was looking at it once more when he suddenly sat up as if he'd been hit in the face. There was this woman going into the loo and her uniform clearly showed CK Tangs on the back. Why was she going to the loo here, and not at her own workplace across the road? Was she playing truant?

The inspector kept on watching and after about ten minutes the same woman was seen leaving the loo, but she was wearing jeans and T-shirt with the same scarf and shades. And she carried a plastic bag.

'Come take a look!' he shouted to the six other officers similarly engaged. 'See? I bet she's got the uniform in the bag,'

Rodrigues remarked.

He then rewound the film and all of them watched the last ten minutes or so in silence.

Initially the copier spewed out fifty copies of one frame, then more frames were blown up and copied. Half an hour later Chong and Dr Wong were looking at the face of a pretty woman wearing large glasses, her head completely covered in a blue-green scarf with geometric patterns, a white T-shirt with no slogan on the front as per usual, well-cut jeans and high heels. A good-looking woman, great shape; could be Chinese, Malay or even Thai.

'Should we put that scarf on the television?' Dr Wong asked.

'I was thinking the same thing, but if they are as professional as we think they are, nothing much will come of it,' said Chong.

'Did you notice the design on the scarf? I don't think it is all that common. Someone must have seen it somewhere. If it is new, maybe the shopkeepers and hawkers will remember it,' said Dr Wong.

'Showing it on the television may be the only way. The police can't possibly talk to every shopkeeper and street hawker, not with the curfew on,' agreed Chong.

'Might be a good idea to get the artists to make a graphic. We must be careful of the words we use when we show it on the television. I suggest that we do not link it to anything particular, just that we would like to speak to anyone who has such a scarf or has seen one like it, for identification purposes. Viewers can take that to mean identification of a bomb victim,' suggested Dr Wong.

'Yes, I see what you mean. A potential informant should not be frightened away.'

★

Asma Latiff was home alone making dinner when she heard the Important Statement about a scarf. She stood rooted to the ground as she heard the description. She felt sick; she must get rid of her scarf right away. Then second thoughts – *there must be others who have the same scarf.* That alone could not be enough. She had to stay calm. *Was there something else to link her to the Bedford?* The telephone had been wiped clean and thrown into a rubbish bin near a bus stand in Scotts Road. *That's it; nothing to worry about.* She could get rid of the scarf in her own time.

Having calmed down, but still in a state of high anxiety, Asma went about preparing dinner; a simple meal of rice and *ikan bilis* (small whitebait), slices of cucumber and the leftover chicken curry. There was ice cream for dessert, and she hoped the children would come home quickly. They were still with Mohammed Ariff's mother; they needn't wait for the curfew to be lifted to cross from one block of flats to another. She telephoned Che Suhaila, and she was told that the children would be home shortly. The old woman also asked Asma if it was true that she had a scarf like the one they were showing on the television. Her daughter, Siti, had said that Asma had, but her son Ridzuan was not so sure. All the children were making up stories that their mothers too had such a scarf. The old woman did not wait for Asma's reaction, but said, 'Not important. I'll send them right over.'

Asma was certain that although she could persuade her daughter that she was mistaken, the other children at Che Suhaila's might tell their parents about what had transpired. There was a risk; but on the other hand, they were all Malays and might not be too keen on talking to the government's *mata-mata* (police).

Chapter Fifteen

All quiet on the front; both sides were waiting for something to happen. Singapore's sorties had obliterated what used to be the Subang and Kuantan air bases. If there were any anti-aircraft batteries in their vicinity they too were history. Radar and imaging techniques proved negative, for there was no sign of the Harriers that had brought down the Chinooks near Mersing, but the nature of the aircraft made it easy to hide in Malaysia's extensive rubber and oil-palm estates. They needed the technical wizardry of another Hawkeye to do a proper sweep.

The Falcons had all gone home, except for the groups cruising the east and west coasts of the Malaysian peninsula in readiness for the return of the aircraft that had been stashed away in Sumatra and in the north, presumably in Thailand. On the ground, the troops of both sides were at a standstill, that is not to say that the guns were silent. The troops stayed in holes in the ground and behind trees and rocks as the heavy guns exchanged fire. Singapore's air power was being held back in the face of superior missiles that the Malaysians were deploying. But behind the hard men of the Malay Regiment were other strong ground forces. If the missiles could continue to keep out the RSAF, Tan Sri Omar was fairly confident that he could indeed drive the aggressor out into the water. That was the key, the missiles and their ability to strike the target despite the enemy's trickery and masking techniques.

He had already made up his mind that the businessman Rajagopal would be rewarded with a Tan Sri in the King's birthday honours list. He had worked out the deal that provided his forces a fighting chance against a clever and technologically advanced enemy. Malaysia had the money, and it was money well spent. Despite all the unfavourable publicity that Malaysia had been assailed with, and China's insulting of Malaysian society, the Americans had seen the justice of the situation and acted accordingly. The money spent was worth it. Definitely.

'So what happens now?' Chong asked Dr Wong and General Woo, the Commander in Chief.

'We have to begin talks, Mr Prime Minister. We are simply hurting each other for no reason, for neither side shows any sign of pulling back. The missiles have complicated the situation for us.'

'That's the name of the game, General. That's war. Expect the unexpected. I am certain that the Americans have a hand in this.'

'The end result has been that my planes are facing great risks, and those risks rise exponentially for the men on the ground. That is why I urge that talks be started quickly, for the sake of both sides. Remember, sir, we have to live with them after this thing is over,' warned Woo.

'I am intensely conscious of that, General. Who should make the first move? We are the pragmatic side... I'm sure you were going to tell me that. Yes, we are.'

'I know this professor in KL who is close to the armed forces and the politicians. Shall I give him a ring? Just exploratory talk. See what he says,' suggested Dr Wong.

'Yes, go ahead, but make clear that you are doing this off your own bat, for the sake of saving lives and finding a long-lasting solution, etc. But water is not negotiable,' said Chong.

'Certainly.'

'Dr Wong, please repeat for the General's benefit what we have learned from studying the outbreak of wars and their outcome in the last twenty years.'

'We have found that, on average, the world experiences thirty major outbreaks of armed conflict every year. And in every case, it has been the party that started the war that benefited from the ultimate settlement. There were two definite exceptions, Iraq and the Punjab rebellion, and possibly the Tamil Tigers insurrection. Some of those wars are still going on. There's one in the Himalayas between Pakistan and India, one in the former Yugoslavia and several in Africa.'

★

Another fearful, steamy night. A brief cloudburst had swept Singapore and Johore at twilight. The men on the front were crouching under plastic as the storm lashed them and shells whizzed over their heads. The ground turned to mud quickly, and the men were beginning to miss the hawkers and the supply trucks. They had to make do with dry rations for the time being.

With the movement in the line, there had also been a movement of the local population. Positions in Jemaluang, Keluang and Batu Pahat had had to be abandoned, and some people, mostly Chinese with some Indians, Sri Lankans and people of other races, had moved south with the Singapore troops, fearing the Malaysians. These people were on the move on foot, and they had to pass the impact areas of Malaysian fire. Heavy casualties were reported and Singapore's medical wing was fully stretched. The problem was that there were no arrangements to receive the refugees when they reached Johore Bahru. The Causeway was broken and the Tuas bridge unusable. The people would have to be accommodated in public facilities such as schools and government buildings in Johore Bahru. But there was no shortage of supplies, for the helicopters kept up a constant supply run.

★

Jaffar Ibrahim and Stella Chin had everything they needed, except electricity. Candles were romantic but without radio and television they were getting no news. Stella had a mobile phone which she used to call her mother and obtain a rough idea of what was going on. But that was not enough; she needed to know more, and she needed help if she was to get out. She decided to make the last ditch call, a number that was to be used only in the direst emergency.

It was indeed the original Ms Choo, who had interviewed her right at the beginning of the great adventure, who answered the phone, and Stella told her she needed to get back to Singapore, with Jaffar Ibrahim. Ms Choo would make arrangements for a military vehicle to collect Stella, but Jaffar Ibrahim was a different matter. He had to stay back. He was on his own. Stella should calm him and promise to return soon, and he should try to speak to the Sultan again. That was important. She should convince Jaffar that she had to be back in Singapore for any number of reasons, from death and injury in the family to obtaining permission from her family to enter into a more lasting relationship with the man. It was left to Stella to choose the path most likely to persuade Jaffar to persist with the Sultan.

'They have promised us great chunks of land around Kota Tinggi, previously owned by people who have run away,' she told Jaffar, his face still flushed from their last bout of love-making.

Without the aircon and even a fan, he was sweating profusely. Stella kept repeating that he must try and see the Sultan before she got back. He was exhausted and he was drowsy; he was half asleep when Stella said, 'It's here,' and walked out of the door quickly.

Jaffar had a glimpse of a jeep before she closed the door behind her, and she was gone. He lay in bed looking up at the ceiling, and even in the state he was in he realised that they were done with him, whoever 'they' were in Singapore. He would never see Stella again, he was sure. But he had no regrets. He would do it all again if a woman like Stella Chin was the reward. But now it was for Jaffar, the consummate politician, to play his hand. He had to build bridges, he had to rehabilitate himself, he must try and see the Sultan. He had a different story to tell.

★

It was Dr Wong Meng Kwang who telephoned Datuk Rahman Malik through the satellite network, Singapore–Hong Kong–Kuala Lumpur. The Professor had been preparing himself to call Dr Wong, and he was particularly pleased that the call had come from the other party.

After the initial pleasantries, Dr Wong told his old acquaintance, 'Datuk, I think it has finally come to pass that we, the forgotten intellectuals, have to stop this unnecessary bloodletting.'

'You think we have any clout when the guns are firing?' exclaimed Datuk.

'Yes, especially now. If we allow one unnecessary death, that is one too many.'

'Singapore started it, you know. I am given to understand that our forces are preparing to launch a major offensive that will take the war right up to Singapore.'

'That will be difficult, but let us not argue about it. Are you in a position to play the role of a go-between? I can obtain such authority for myself from the Singapore side. If you are similarly placed we might be able to initiate contacts that could lead to talks of some sort to settle this thing.'

'Yes, I think I can obtain such authority, for I am on friendly terms with Tan Sri Omar and the Prime Minister, but I get the feeling that you are suggesting some sort of a settlement without Singapore forces actually going back to Singapore.'

'Singapore forces are prepared to move back a bit more, but I am afraid that the final line of control will include parts of Johore Bahru and all the water catchment areas.'

'That is a difficult proposal for me to take to Tan Sri Omar,' said Datuk.

'But that could easily be the starting point of talks between our two sides. As I understand it, you want us out of Johore and we want the water. That can be the basis of negotiations, even consideration of a cash component for an outright purchase of the territory. Worth thinking about and talking about, what do you think?' asked Wong.

'How much?'

Dr Wong said, laughing; 'We can work that out. The exact area, the commercial value, if there is arable land, a nominal value for the mud flats, and so on. I can't put a specific figure on it, but there are precedents. The Louisiana Settlement, the California acquisition, Alaska, and so on. But no seller, if I may use the term, was considered to have done a bad deal. They were all equitable deals and I am sure we can arrive at a fair settlement in this case. We want our water resources, that is the main thing.'

'And JB?'

Dr Wong said, laughing again: 'An ambit claim, but really the line of control will include the pipelines and that will take a chunk of JB. Yes, we can place urban values on that part.'

'I will telephone and make an appointment to see Tan Sri Omar and the Perdana Mentri. But I doubt they would welcome any talk of surrendering land for money. I will try.'

'Will you call me, or should I call you?'

'I will call you. *Selamat Petang.*'

'Good night, Datuk.'

★

'The game's afoot,' Dr Wong announced to no one in particular.

Steven Chong, meanwhile, was being briefed by police on their investigations and a surprising telephone call that they had received from a child about some other child's mother having a scarf like the one described on television. The child had been interrupted and the call terminated before a trace could be made. But it was a Malay child, which persuaded investigators that it could be genuine. But then it was mostly Malay women who wore scarves, and the link was fairly obvious to make.

'Tell them to look at surveillance film further afield from the explosion sites,' Steven Chong told his police liaison officer, Deputy Superintendent Max Kam. 'These films, the scarf and the telephones... you see, the clues are there. We just have to keep looking and digging. I want the full history of those phones dug up. I know the phone company says these records are buried under millions of other records, but we have to see them.'

'We have provided the telephone company with some of our own people for the job. They are digging. I believe they have gone back three years, and not one call was made from these phones in that time. It is much more difficult to see if any calls were made to those numbers, that is why it is taking so much time. Every number that we know of has to be put through a trace. International calls are relatively easy, but there does not appear to have been any to those five numbers. In addition, that woman's photograph from the cinema surveillance camera is being put through a complicated photofit device. It is a slow and cumbersome procedure. The American company that we have contracted for the job is saying that the specific details are so few that they can name a million women as fitting this face. But we will keep looking,' said Kam.

The radio played a new song, said to be popular with NS men. A new group calling itself the Serangoon Garden A Cappella Singers had burst on to the scene with what was described as 'the soldier's song'. Dave Mitchell laughed out loud when he heard the title, *Lilly Mei-Lin*. But it had a certain charm. And it began with the words,

> *Under the moonlight*
> *On the Mersing beach…*

The words could already be heard from the long lines of troop-carrying trucks that filled the streets. *Lilly* was going to be a hit. Every soldier's home should have a CD, and that was almost every home in Singapore, with its universal national service.

★

The island remained under curfew, and Dr Wong was aware of the damage it was doing to Singapore's international standing.

'The curfew is doing us more damage than any bombings,' he remarked to the Prime Minister.

'I am aware of that, Dr Wong. I want to persuade Suleiman to come to the conference table. We have to start somewhere. As a first step, can we suggest a ceasefire?'

'I can call my old friend, the Professor. He hasn't got back to me after our last conversation, and they might take it as another sign of weakness if I phoned him. He needs a prompt.'

General Woo was on the line, with a suggestion for Chong to think over, and the Prime Minister put him on the loudspeaker so other members could hear him.

'We haven't really used our navy so far,' Woo said. 'We could move them in formation up the east coast. Give Omar something to think about. If the Malaysians dared show their Harriers again they will be blown out of the sky, because my ships will have superior air cover and we have some really good missile frigates. Forgive me for thinking aloud, but we can take along a couple of empty ships dressed up as troop carriers, and we could try and persuade them that another invasion was in the pipeline. They still have some of those missiles, and they could do some damage without exposing their aircraft, but we can move the convoy beyond the range of their missiles.'

'How quickly can you move?' asked Chong.

'I can get the navy to get the ships together within a couple of hours. There are plenty of empty civilian ships we can choose from. I would say the convoy can be moving within three or four hours of your agreement,' said Woo.

'I need ten minutes to get the members' approval. Go ahead on that tentative basis.'

'You can provide the clearance to our liaison man. I will be issuing commands and signing papers for the next half hour or so.'

'Thank you, General.'

'There are some big teeth left in the old lion yet.'

'Yes, of course. Goodbye.'

★

Datuk Rahman was furious.

'I thought we had an understanding. Bringing in your navy is a provocation and an escalation,' he said icily to Dr Wong.

'But you were to call me. I have little influence on the military, you know that. When you failed to call me, they read it as meaning that all bets were off. May I suggest that I try and persuade the military to halt all naval activity in return for a cease-fire? You must appreciate that has to be the first step to holding talks.'

'While you are still squatting on our land?' asked the Datuk.

'I can assure you that the present line of control is temporary. We will pull back substantially if there is agreement on the water resources,' said Dr Wong, firmly.

'What do you mean by *substantially*?'

'We wish to retain just enough of the mainland to protect our water supply.'

'Can I convey all this to the General and the Perdana Mentri?'

the Datuk asked.

'Yes, in this sequence. First a ceasefire, to include land, air and sea, to be followed by contacts between our High Commissioners at a neutral site. Things can progress from there.'

'You didn't mention the money part.'

'We don't have to go into all that at this stage. The negotiators can work it out as part of a final settlement. You just talk to them and tell me when you want the ceasefire to go into effect and both sides can make announcements. In the meantime, remember, it would be a criminal waste of human life if anyone gets killed between now and the formal announcement,' said Dr Wong.

'I agree, but it cuts both ways. Anyway, let us hope for the best.'

Steven Chong was elated. A mutually agreed ceasefire came into effect at midnight. Tan Sri Omar cancelled a paratroop drop on JB's Senai airport, a bold move that would have split the Singapore forces if it had succeeded. General Woo recalled his naval flotilla, but a couple of missile-armed frigates hung off the Mersing coast.

The first contact between the two sides was to be in Bangkok the following morning when their respective ambassadors were to meet in the office of the Thai Prime Minister. At 12.05 a.m. an Important Statement on the television announced that the curfew was lifted as of that moment.

'And I repeat, a cease fire is in effect and the curfew has been lifted,' Ms Fonseca announced, her voice cracking with emotion.

Lights were coming on all over the island. People were coming out on to the streets, the traffic was building up and, with special permission, all the nightclubs were opening. Families were getting together. The cathedrals, churches, temples, and mosques were all being opened. Thankful prayers were accompanied by prayers for the souls of the dead. But elsewhere, Singapore was in celebratory mood. They understood perfectly the implications of the ceasefire without the withdrawal of troops.

'The Singapore Lion has roared,' Chong, flushed with excitement, told the Blue Room in emergency session.

And he received the obligatory *Roar! Roar! Roar!* in return. 'Go home and get some sleep, gentlemen. It's a different game from now on.'

★

Dave Mitchell announced 'The war is over!' even before the announcement on the television.

He woke up Dom and Tessy who were beginning to doze off with all that scotch inside them. The television switched to a repeat of the previous year's National Day celebrations. The great city was alive again.

Chapter Sixteen

Daybreak.

Dom, Tessy and Dave, walking to the city centre, were struck by the movement in the streets. The heavy traffic was matched on the pavement by people taking in the sights on foot, like themselves.

'It is the new dawn,' Dave told Dom, as Tessy pointed the way to a stall where you could get *bak kut teh* (a stew made of pork bones) for breakfast. Buses, taxis and the MRT were coming on stream; but except for that the city had been up and about since the curfew ended. There were crowds of people outside city buildings, waiting for their offices to open.

'Look at them,' Dave remarked. 'Can't wait to get back to work. Today is the first day of the rest of their lives. If you've got any money, buy shares. Just buy. Anything. Everything will be going up. I can't really put a cap on it at this moment.'

'What are your plans now?' asked Tessy.

'I'll check into the nearest hotel. I am sure the airport will be opening, if it has not already, but I want to stay here a few more days,' said Dave.

'Unfinished business?' asked Dom.

'In a manner of speaking, yes,' admitted Dave.

Dave was a very rich man, and he knew that. But this girl, Jacinta, had been on his brain the last few days. He thought he had got over her, but all the while he was cooped up by the curfew she had been on his mind. When he slept she was in his dreams.

'Dom, please toss this coin. I want to call.'

Dom did, and Dave said, 'Heads.'

'You called right,' Dom said.

Dave grabbed him and hugged him. Dom said, 'Easy, easy. This is Singapore, they don't go in for that sort of thing. Does this mean I can keep your coin?'

'You helped me make up my mind. Let's have fun. I am going to arrange a very special dinner for ten people. Something you'll remember for a long time,' said Dave.

'Ten who?' enquired Dom.

'Tessy and Rose, you and your partner, I and my partner, plus my friend Paul Kemp and partner, and my friend Simon Tay and partner,' said Dave.

'Your partner?' asked Tessy.

'Yes, my partner. Her name is Jacinta, Jacinta Kishen Lal. I might marry her.'

'Good on you, mate. But I am afraid I don't have a partner for the occasion,' said Dom.

'I am sure Freddie can organise something.'

'I have given up on that. He hasn't met one who can keep up with him. Dom, tell him what you told me about *Lolita*,' prompted Tessy.

'What about Lolita?'

'He says he is going to be a great writer like Nabokov, the guy who wrote *Lolita*. Come on Dom, you tell him.'

Eating the *bak kut teh* with *teh-tarek* (tea in a long glass with a lot of froth) on the side, Dom expounded his dream, based on his own limited knowledge of literature and authors. The one that had captured his imagination was Vladimir Nabokov.

'He was a Russian, brought up and educated in Germany with English as a second language, and he went on to become a great writer in English. After the war he found himself in Paris and he wrote some very fine, deep novels, but none made any money. He finally became tired of the hunger and the cold and determined to make some money before he could give the world the benefit of any more of his heavy, serious stuff. He was going to play games with the English language and tell an improbable yet erotic story to make them buy his book. And he sat down and started his book, the first lines were: *The tip of the tongue taking a trip down the palate to tap at three the back of my teeth. Lolita.* The rest, as they say, is history.

'By the way, those opening words were to provide an example of how the power of the English language could be harnessed by maintaining a rhythm, or beat, as he explains later in the book.

Anyone can do that.'

'See? He's even memorised the words. And he is seeing a Nabokov parallel with himself,' said Tessy.

'Maybe, maybe not, but I'd say I won't know whether I can or not unless I try,' said Dom.

'Good on you, mate. At least you won't die wondering,' Dave said.

★

In Palembang, like many others that had served as a port in the storm, the temporary refugees were all trying to get back to Singapore. David Russell called three of his senior men at home and told them to pass on his advice to all their corporate clients for the whole day: 'Buy, buy, buy, and don't let the profit-takers give you cold feet! Look on the long-term.'

Similarly, Ossie Eisenberg farmed out his 'buy' orders, and Peter Chapman called Elizabeth of the big butt and told her that she was authorised to approve lending for stocks and shares for the A-list of their customers, until midday. He was expecting a decline in the afternoon because of profit-takers, but any further lending must await his return. Then all six, Leslie and David, Patricia and Ossie, and Connie and Peter went to the waterfront to try and find transport back to Singapore.

'There are only two flights to Singapore out of Palembang and both are full with a waiting list as long as your arm,' the travel agent told Peter. 'Try and find a boat.'

★

Kernail Singh came home with his head in bandages; a tiny piece of shrapnel had cost him his left eye, but there wasn't another mark on him. He had always been reluctant to explain to his family and friends what he did in the army, creating images of all sorts of gung-ho action. And now with an eye gone, and his great physique, he presented an irresistible picture of manhood. He never told them that all he did was load shells into a gun and that a shell burst some distance away had sent that single piece of lethal metal into his eye as he had leapt for cover.

He walked tall, smiling at the admiring glances. He was quick to persuade his brother to allow his sister to marry her Canadian pilot, then he himself arranged for a taxi to take him to see Monica Tham. Tony Cadenza was back from the wars, a great hero, looking like Moshe Dayan in his better days, and he had the world in his hands. Just think what he could have done if had *both* those melting eyes.

★

The first contact between Malaysian and Singaporean officials in the Thai Prime Minister's office was followed by a surprising offer from the American ambassador to host further talks on the *Truman* with larger delegations, to be followed by the presence of the two Prime Ministers for the signing of the agreement. But a signing ceremony was thought to be a long way off, considering the difficulties in assessing land values and marking out the water catchment areas. But the Americans were adamant that a peace agreement be arrived at quickly. The long and twisted Middle East peace negotiations had taken a heavy toll on their patience. In actual fact, the line that Singapore wanted drawn had long been measured and mapped by their army technicians. They had been tramping south Johore with their theodolites for some years and they could place the markers within a day; they also had in mind more permanent structures which, too, they could put up very quickly, sealing off all contact between the two sides in the newly acquired territory and thus removing any areas of friction. The water catchment areas were to be out of bounds to all civilians, Singaporeans and unwilling Malaysian residents alike.

The line started on the beach near a village called Tanjong Lembu and dropped south with a few bends, covering all the catchment areas, then enclosing the pumping station and following the pipes through JB town to the water's edge, including the railway line and the Causeway itself. New pipes were to be laid east of the line.

'That's going to cost you,' Datuk Rahman told Dr Wong when he heard about it.

'We have the money, but more importantly, Datuk, that's the only way to make sure that we don't leave behind any loose ends for more trouble in the future,' Dr Wong told him. 'All that area on our side of the demarcation line on the Peninsula will be depopulated over time and given over to the Water Department and military installations. The other part of town will be encouraged to focus on the other crossing, for we are determined to rebuild it, and even add another crossing later on. That way the Causeway will lose its importance to the civilian population. It will devolve into purely military and technical use.'

★

James Roderick Johnson was in consideration for the plum job of Ambassador to Japan. Among the shining achievements on his CV was the fact that he had finally persuaded the Singaporeans to buy the upgraded, revamped Patriot anti-missile system. The Malaysians were to continue their missile purchases, and in addition the Malaysians had agreed to restructure their air force entirely around the new F-14s, F-16s and F-18s, although they also intended to keep the Harriers. The whole thing had to be concluded quickly so he could leave for bigger things on other shores. *This guy Cohen had proved to be extremely useful; might take him along to Tokyo if they will let me.* Cohen himself would be only too happy, for the Tokyo posting was in the senior grade. It was to be hoped that Cohen would come away clean; this woman Janet might not be appropriate for him in the Tokyo environment. That would be his choice, of course. In any case, Janet's loyalties were to Singapore. He, Johnson, would love to be a fly on the wall when Cohen finally made the break. The devious nature of mankind never failed to amaze him.

★

Without urging, members of the Blue Room reconvened before midday, although Steven Chong had expected them to sleep well and report back in the evening. Dr Wong had not gone home at all, a short nap in an annexe was all that he needed to return to his

176

bouncy, bounding self. Just to keep them amused, he slipped easily into the role he was noted for among friends, that of raconteur. As Steven Chong conferred with his army, air force, navy, Special Branch and Internal Security aides and advisers, Dr Wong took the mike:

'Good morning, gentlemen, for it is not noon yet. Let me, first of all, bring to your attention two famous quotes. On a wall in Belfast there used to be an IRA pronouncement which said, *History is written by the winner*. Perfectly true, as the Americans and the British have demonstrated so consistently. So our writers are busy rewriting the history of South-East Asia with Malaysia. My next quote is from Dan Quayle in 1990 when he was Vice-President of the United States. His exact words were, *If we do not succeed, then we run the risk of failure*. Brilliant, don't you think?'

Loud laughter.

They loved it; anything that brought the Americans down a notch always seemed to find willing ears. Was it really just envy?

'Now, let me tell you how they used to treat various territories so casually in the old days. The stories about Malacca and Hong Kong are well known, so I will cast my net a little further out.

'When Charles the Second of England married Catherine of Braganza in the Sixteenth century, her father, John the Fourth of Portugal, gave a dowry of various parts of the world. One of these was Bombay. Imagine that: the British got Bombay, or Mumbai, and all the islands that city is built on as part of their queen's dowry. They didn't ask the locals what they thought of it. Then, at the same time, at the height of the spice discoveries, James the First of England also assumed the title of King of Pulo Run and Pulo Ai. Pulo was a corruption of *pulau*, meaning *island*. These are tiny islands, four kilometres by one kilometre, in the Moluccas. Their claim to fame was that they were the only places on earth where you could find nutmeg in those days. How do you explain that there was no nutmeg anywhere else on earth except on these two islands, but that was the fact. The first Europeans who came across nutmeg were simply enthralled. They bought all they could carry and they sold them at a profit of three thousand and two hundred per cent in Europe. The British Chancellor is said to have assessed the value of Run and Ai to the Crown as exceeding that of Scotland.'

Steven Chong was now ready to speak to his peers, and Dr Wong bowed out.

'Yes, gentlemen, the Lion has roared and all our strategic analysts agree that we are on the way to succeeding in everything we set out to do. Yes, there was a price to pay, and some of us feel that pain more than others. I extend my heartfelt condolences to every member who has suffered grievous loss or serious injury to a member of his family. We knew the risks and what the stakes were when we set out on this great enterprise, and sometimes we need to be reminded of the old saying: no pain, no gain.

'But we as a people are the stronger for it. We have earned our manhood, we have survived the rites of passage to a more glorious future. Like the Americans who value their freedom with a greater fervour than is normally the case, because they had to fight for it, we too will now value our freedom and independence more. That will be the foundation to create greater loyalty and commitment among our young people. They know now that the good life they enjoy has been fought and won the hard way, that a price has been paid in blood, that a similar price may have to be paid in the future if their survival is threatened. There are the negotiations to be conducted with the Malaysians, but they already know what the parameters are. All they can do now is to try and extort as much money as they can from us. That is the limit of the options that they have, apart from minor details such as moving a territory marker a few feet here or a few feet there. But nothing will be allowed to intrude into the integrity of Water Board operations and the area they require. Let us, therefore, be thankful and joyful. Do I hear a roar?'

The members were suddenly brought back to earth from the reverie created by the Prime Minister's rosy picture.

Roar! Roar! Roar!

'Let's go out and celebrate,' an upstanding pillar of the Hokkien community said, and Steven Chong was quick to dampen any public display of elation.

'Careful, gentlemen, I don't want the Malaysians to feel as though they have lost the war. It could be counter-productive if that destabilised Suleiman Bakri's already shaky regime. It is for that reason that I have specifically told all organisations to desist from public celebrations. *We* know we have won – that is enough. If you wish to celebrate, do it discreetly behind closed doors. The face we wish to present to the Malaysians, especially General Omar, is one of relief, exactly the same as what they must be feeling. Suleiman Bakri will be telling his people that he has decided to sell a load of mud at the price of gold. Let them believe that, if they want to. As for ourselves, we will be buying mud at the going rate for mud, but we have the expertise to raise its value to the level of gold.

'It will, of course, take time, but all that area will get the Dutch treatment. We will have land and we will have plenty of fresh water. I am extremely confident of a final and peaceful settlement because I feel that where there is money involved, people can be persuaded to be amenable to our requirements. We will meet again when we have an indication from our negotiators what the terms of the final agreement are likely to be. You probably know already that the markets are all up, even across the Causeway. Go out and grab your share of our good fortune.'

Roar! Roar! Roar!

★

By lunchtime, the *Truman* had deposited all its refugees back in Singapore, and all the other diplomats were expected to be back on station before the end of the day. But the civilians who took boats and sampans to Indonesian ports were finding it difficult to find return transport. Boats were going out from Singapore and charging double, so it was almost midnight when the Chapmans, Russells and the Eisenbergs finally made it back.

'We should not have gone further than Bintan,' Peter Chapman remarked. 'Only thirty minutes away.'

'But that's too close to the action, if there was going to be any,' his wife, Connie, said. 'I think we did the right thing.'

When they got back Singapore was already celebrating, the restaurants and shops and clubs were all open. They all seemed to have overlooked their old closing times and appeared to be bent on staying open all hours to make up for the curfew.

★

Dave Mitchell had promised that the dinner he was organising for the following night would be quite something.

'It would be a terrible waste if you can't find a partner for Dom,' he phoned to tell Tessy, who, meanwhile, was organising another party for the Saturday night.

Almost all the places were booked out, but Peng Ah Pat, the *wayang* lover, found a place in Pasir Ris, the Blue Orchid, which also had karaoke.

'There will be fifteen of us, give or take one,' Tessy told Peng and the booking was confirmed. Dave Mitchell was paying for that, too.

As soon as that was done, Dom called Dave at the hotel.

'What's so special about your dinner?' he asked Dave, who had been out the whole day visiting various hotels.

He had a menu with him, he explained, and he wanted to find someone who could do it, hang the expense. He wanted it done exactly as stated in the menu, including the wines, which were all Australian.

'I found one guy who could do it, but he named two other chefs he wanted to help out.'

'What exactly are you ordering?' Dom asked him.

'It's like this, mate. Some time ago I was reading a newspaper and I saw this menu someone had prepared that was said to be a prizewinner. I cut it out and kept it in my wallet, and I told myself that when I made the grade I'd have the same thing. I have made the grade. This war worked for me,' said Dave.

'What exactly did you do?'

'Sell some planes; but seriously, it is better if you don't know too much. Military sales are always a touchy subject, depending on who you are with.'

'Is it safe to keep your company?' asked Dom.

'Absolutely,' asserted Dave.

'If you say so. What's the menu like?'

'That will be a surprise. But you better get on with finding a partner for tomorrow night. I am making the booking for ten. There'll be an empty seat if you don't have a partner.'

Chapter Seventeen

Dave Mitchell was in an elegant suit, and standing beside him was a striking woman who was almost as tall as himself. She was wearing a full-length navy blue silk dress with a thigh-high cut on the left.

They stepped forward to greet Tessy, Rose and Dom as they walked up into the lobby.

'Jacinta, my friends Freddie and Rose, and this is Dom from Melbourne.'

Right at that minute Tessy's face lit up as a woman in a light green ensemble reached them.

'My beautiful cousin Roslyn,' he announced as he planted a kiss on her cheek.

She wore loose slacks with a half-sleeve blouse, a thick belt, and a thin chain with a tiny cross on it. She had three rings on her right hand. Rose, who was in a Chinese-style green satin *samfoo* top and black slacks, was also quick to hug and kiss her.

'Nice outfit,' she said.

Dave suggested that they could move to the bar to wait for the others or they could remain in the lobby, for they should arrive at any moment.

They did, soon enough, together, although they had come separately.

Dave introduced them. Simon Tay was in the Singapore forces, but he didn't have to wear a uniform, meaning he was in intelligence. His wife, Angela, in cream slacks with a bright blue shantung top, was in the Education Ministry. Paul Kemp worked in the Australian High Commission in some unstated capacity. His wife, Joanne, a secretary in the High Commission, was a smallish, dark-haired woman with startling, iceberg-blue eyes. She wore a black cocktail dress with a largish diamond on a thin gold chain. And that made up Dave's ten; Dom and Roslyn were now a couple for the sake of the dinner.

The small function room of the New Century was decorated in off-white wallpaper with gold trim. There were huge bowls of orchids in the corners near the wall and between them a large mirror with an imitation Louis XIV frame in full gilt.

Dave had given some thought to the seating arrangement. He sat at the head and Jacinta faced him at the other end. On Dave's right, Jacinta's left, Dom was at the top followed by Rose, Simon and Joanne. On the other side, Tessy was at the top followed by Roslyn, Paul and Angela.

'Gentlemen, I arrived at this configuration for the seating specifically to encourage conversation,' Dave said.

Simon followed quickly with, 'And the first rule is going to be that we stay away from military jargon, such as *configuration*.'

There were embossed place names with little Aussie flags in the corners, and the menus were similarly decorated.

The menu read like this:

Assorted Canapés
1996 Tyrrells Vat 47 Pinot Chardonnay

Cold Soup of Eggplant
Avocado with Caviar
Krug 1989

Marinated Tuna with Goat's Cheese, Roasted Capsicum and Rocket
Roasted NZ Scampi seasoned with Tea
Scampi Oil Grilled Eel on Sushi Rice
1995 Petaluma Riesling

Confit of Tasmanian Ocean Trout with Unpasteurised Ocean Trout Roe,
Braised Red Capsicum, Leeks, Konbu, Capers and Parsley Oil
1993 Tyrrells Vat 1 Semillon
1989 Tyrrells Vat 1 Semillon

Grilled Fillet of Veal with Wasabi and Sea Urchin Butter
1996 Coldstream Hills Reserve
Pinot Noir

Roasted Deboned Rack of Australian Lamb with Braised Witlof and Miso
Sauce

1989 Penfold's Grange

Flourless Chocolate Cake
Bitter Chocolate Sorbet
Orange Ice Cream
Seppelt Rutherglen Tokay DP 57

Dave noticed that his guests were literally dumbfounded when they had finished reading the menu.

'I told you you'd never forget this little meal,' Dave said smugly.

'Little meal, he says,' Paul remarked.

'This is going to cost you a packet. They must have gone to some trouble to get these Australian wines.'

'Yes, they did,' Dave said, with a wide grin.

'So you made a motza out of this war,' Simon said quietly, casually.

But he realised instantly that he was stating the obvious. No confirmation was necessary. Well, his people would be very interested, but unfortunately the drama was over, bar some minor cleaning up. And that did not include people like Dave Mitchell, who would be in the shadows of every war, playing every side. *Useful to know, for the future,* he told himself.

But Dave had picked up his remark, and said, equally casually, that anti-missile systems were expensive things which needed expensive maintenance. Simon's uncle was known to be big in that sort of thing; and he was one of those trusted people around the Prime Minister.

Paul laughed, but said nothing, although he had a brother-in-law in the missile business in America.

'War means money,' Dave said. 'If you are smart you'll pick up some.'

'What about the suffering? And the death and mutilation?' asked Roslyn.

'That's the sad part, once the genie is out of the bottle. The point is not to engage in war at all. But if that becomes unavoidable, then baser instincts come into play,' said Simon.

'Yes, Roslyn, there is nothing worse than war in human experience. But once nationalism comes into play, even the crudest 'jingoistic talk will find favour,' agreed Jacinta.

'But there's always money to be made in war. I believe Japan's economic recovery was mainly due to the Korean War,' said Dom.

'Hey, I know people who became very rich because of the Korean War. Our rubber price and tin price all shot up, and the Americans were ordering all sorts of other things from Singapore, like barbed wire, electrical fittings and plastic things,' Rose said.

'The Vietnam War had a similar effect on the economies of many countries in the region, Singapore especially. In another time, it is not a secret that the Rothschilds in Paris became rich by successively financing wars,' put in Joanne.

'I am sure there are other people who do the same,' suggested Angela.

'The British and the Dutch used to set up trading companies in which their respective kings held substantial shares. Then there were the privateers, really just pirates given the blessing to attack and loot the ships of their enemies,' said Paul.

'Yes, Drake springs to mind,' agreed Dave.

The food and the wines moved on at a sedate pace, considering they had a lot of ground to cover before they reached the Tokay DP 57.

'I've never eaten goat's cheese before,' Angela remarked.

It was the roe that struck Joanne.

'Hmmm, unpasteurised,' she said.

The sea urchin butter needed to be explained to Rose before she would touch it.

Dave and Jacinta watched in satisfaction as their guests plodded on.

It was a full three hours later that they finally reached the lamb with witlof and miso sauce and, surprisingly, that was polished off quite easily, in anticipation of the desserts.

'Just desserts,' Joanne said.

'Yeah, yeah,' they all responded.

Dave scribbled a few words on a menu and asked Dom to pass it on to Jacinta. It said, simply: *Je t'aime toujours, XXX.*

The next morning Tessy told Dom that Roslyn had been impressed by his reserve, for he had studiously refrained from his customary rude jokes; but Roslyn had whispered to Tessy before she went off to her car: 'Tell him I have no intention of leaving Singapore under any circumstances.'

'You know what that means? The ball is in your court,' said Tessy.

'I have to go back to Australia,' said Dom.

'Whatever. It's your decision. Anyway, let me tell you this much. She is a widow, a highly respected executive secretary in a multinational company, with a son in national service and a daughter doing her A levels. You can take it from there, or you can go back to your cold, miserable city, alone.'

'Who's coming to the party tonight?'

'All right, change the topic. The whole gang will be there. Only Ching Quee is in doubt.'

'Even Larry?' asked Dom.

'Even Larry Lim and his wife. I have a surprise for them,' said Tessy, mysteriously.

And so it was that the old gang met up again at the Blue Orchid in Pasir Ris. Only Dave and Jacinta were the new faces. Tessy and Rose had arrived early so Dom could greet all his old friends. First to arrive after them were Peng and his young wife Daisy, who was now trying to make it as a Canto-pop singer.

'Wayang very difficult, lah,' she said, as Peng showed her off with obvious pride.

She wore a cheongsam, unusual for a time of Paris chic and London cool. She had classical features with a high forehead.

'I'm sorry to hear about your wife,' Peng whispered to Dom as they watched Raymond Choo approach them with arms wide open.

Beaming, he introduced his wife, Sui Cheng, wearing an olive green silk dress and a diffident manner suited to the wife of a senior bureaucrat, now former.

'I got three kids, man,' he said. 'Luckily Sui Cheng is not working, so she got time to make sure they don't play the fool, ah?'

And Sui Cheng just smiled, but she looked unhappy that he had let on that she was not working.

'Aiyah, Raymond, they will think I'm lazy.'

'No woman who stays home to look after the children can be

called lazy. We all know it's hard work,' said Raymond.

'Okay, okay. But you don't have to broadcast to everyone,' said Sui Cheng.

Dom thought the little exchange could have gone a bit further, but for the arrival of Rahmat Majid and his new wife, Soraya. She was new to all of them, and they all shook hands.

'You got taste, you old wag,' Peng whispered to Rahmat as Rose congratulated the Kelantan beauty on her exquisite batik outfit. Just then Dave and Jacinta arrived, both taller than anyone else there. Jacinta wore a mauve top with designer jeans and a large, thick belt and chunky necklace to match. They went over to every couple there and introduced themselves and chatted a while.

'Seasoned party-goers,' Rose remarked.

'More than that: good manners,' Tessy said.

Sam arrived next with his tall, beautiful wife, Helen, who appeared to be a little self-conscious that she was taller than Sam. She wore a cream suit, and no heels.

'How come we never met before, ah?' Rose wondered as she took her by the hand and introduced her to everybody else.

And no one mentioned The Lost-Neck Monster.

The last to arrive was Larry and the plump, bouncy Aileen. He had put on hardly any weight at all, but he had an obvious bald patch in the centre of his scalp. The other men carried the years on their faces, and all had studiously kept their weight down.

'We're having *dian xin* cuisine, that's new here since your time. All *halal* for Rahmat's sake,' Peng said, since he was the one who had made the booking.

Dom told Dave it was actually *yum-cha* and *dim sum*, as is common in Australia.

'Today, ah, please make an exception, and I want all of you to eat well in honour of our guests. So no dieting today, okay?'

They had two rectangular tables pulled together, with four seats to a side. Tessy and Dom with Rose between them took the side nearest the wall, the empty seat for Ching Quee if he turned up. On their left was Raymond and Sui Cheng, and Helen and Sam. The foursome opposite Dom was made up of Dave and Jacinta, Peng and Daisy. The other side was made up of Rahmat and Soraya, Larry and Aileen.

'I'm so happy today,' Larry said. 'I can still see us going to the Bukit Bintang park in KL all those years ago. Remember the gaming tables? You people don't know, but we, Dom and I, were actually banned from playing there.'

Aileen was giggling, all her fat jiggling.

'He told me everything,' she said, 'but that was before he met me, so I forgive him. He's cute.'

You could see the happiness in Larry's face. The more she giggled and jiggled her bosom, the more he beamed with pride. Dave and Jacinta, of course, didn't know about Larry's strange love affair with fat, so they appeared amused at Aileen's antics. The others carried on as if nothing was the matter.

Helen asked Sui Cheng about her children, Jacinta told Soraya they were leaving for Paris the next day and Rose asked Raymond about 'the arrangements'. Everything was ready, she was told. Then she said, loudly, so all could hear: 'Hey, Larry-ah, we got a nice surprise for you.'

Larry and Aileen asked at the same time, 'What?'

'It won't be a surprise if I told you, right?' said Rose.

'We have karaoke here. Wanna have a go?' Dom asked Dave.

Dave looked at Jacinta, and she nodded.

★

When Dave walked up to the mike, hardly anyone bothered to even look up from their dumplings, except for his own group. When the first bars struck up, some people in the packed restaurant realised that it was a Mandarin song and watched in amusement, because surely the *ang-moh* was going to butcher it.

When he started singing, Dom realised what a miracle it really was: a Caucasian voice taking the twists and turns of Mandarin in perfect pitch and harmony, and it had the desired effect. The entire restaurant fell silent, as the tall man whispered the words of love, as if into the ears of his own sweetheart.

When he finished, many people stood up to applaud, not just the people at his own table. Jacinta was a proud woman as her eyes followed him making his way back.

What? A request? Dave walked back to the mike, and it was going to be a duet. The woman who took her place beside him, nodded to him with a smile, and they sang together beautifully.

When it was over, she gave him her card and told him in English: 'Some day, maybe we can do it again.'

Dave said, 'I hope so, and thank you,' and made his way back.

Sam took the card and quickly announced that it was a Hong Kong singer who had been well-known some years ago, but who had got married and settled down and faded out of the singing scene.

'Maybe she's planning a comeback,' he said, 'and a duet with a Caucasian would be a good gimmick.'

'Well, it's not going to work. I am out of the scene tomorrow,' Dave said.

They had almost done the menu, after the shark's fin dumpling soup, the Shanghai steamed dumpling, the water-chestnut dumpling soup and the deep-fried shrimp roll, when a waitress came up to whisper in Rose's ear. Then Rose announced, 'Ladies and gentlemen, a special presentation.'

It was the most incredible show they had ever seen. It was the lovely Lingling, all pink and round and jolly, bouncing on to the small stage area where the karaoke was, with those famous words, 'So you want to see fat little pigsy dance, ah?'

She joked, rolled on the ground, she sang a few verses of a witty song, she laughed a lot, and then she said goodbye, reminding her fans that they could see more of her on the Internet.

All along everyone had avoided looking at Larry. His face was all screwed up and he appeared to be struggling with himself. Aileen hung on to his hand. Finally, she said softly to Tessy, 'Please call an ambulance.'

He pulled out his mobile and got on to it, as Dom requested everyone to stay where they were and not to crowd around him. Aileen had his head in her lap, and she stroked his forehead as she whispered in his ear.

It took ten minutes for the ambulance to arrive, then she handed him over to them and wept quietly. They gave him two injections and worked on him for about half an hour before they could move him. Aileen said thank you and goodnight and accompanied Larry to hospital.

'We have to finish the programme,' Peng said. 'We may not get the chance again.'

They were serving the *mala*, or roast chicken with spicy Sichuan sauce, as Peng went behind the karaoke stage and emerged with a cumbersome hi-fi set, circa 1958.

'Now listen, ladies and gentlemen,' he said. 'See how we leap across time.'

He put on the record, and *The Portuguese Fisherman's Daughter*, a bit scratchy, found willing admirers again.

Rose held Tessy's hand, Daisy smiled at Peng, Raymond squeezed Sui Cheng's hand, Helen leaned closer to Sam, Rahmat gazed on his young beauty who lowered her eyes, Dave leaned over and kissed Jacinta on the cheek, and Dom wept.

★

Samsuddin Salleh finished writing a speech for Suleiman Bakri, then sat in front of a large map of Johore with a magnifying glass. He followed the new red line, bisecting Johore Bahru slightly west of the Causeway, which suddenly was part of Singapore. But that was not his concern at this time. He located a small village, still in Malaysian territory, and the small rivulet that went past it, and his face softened for the first time since this nasty business began.

He put together a large hamper with biscuits and chocolates, a tin each of Ovaltine, Milo and Horlicks, two tinned cakes and an envelope with 1,000 ringgit, then he summoned his driver, and they were on the road immediately. They would reach the village by dawn and catch his friend before he left the house. They made good time; then, after the usual greetings, and with the driver trailing them with the hamper, the two old men set out on the familiar journey, past the tapioca and sweet potato patches, the rambutan and papaya trees, the clump of banana, the durian plantation, and finally the sugarcane on the waterside. Then the two men ceremoniously urinated into the little stream.

For the final act, Samsuddin took the hamper from the driver and presented it to his old friend, and turned for the car as the *Selamat Jalan,* Safe Journey, rang in his ear. They might never meet again, Samsuddin knew, but he was smiling. *For Samsuddin Salleh does not forgive or forget.*